Avoid alcohol
OPEN
CLOSE
Push down & turn
I0716702

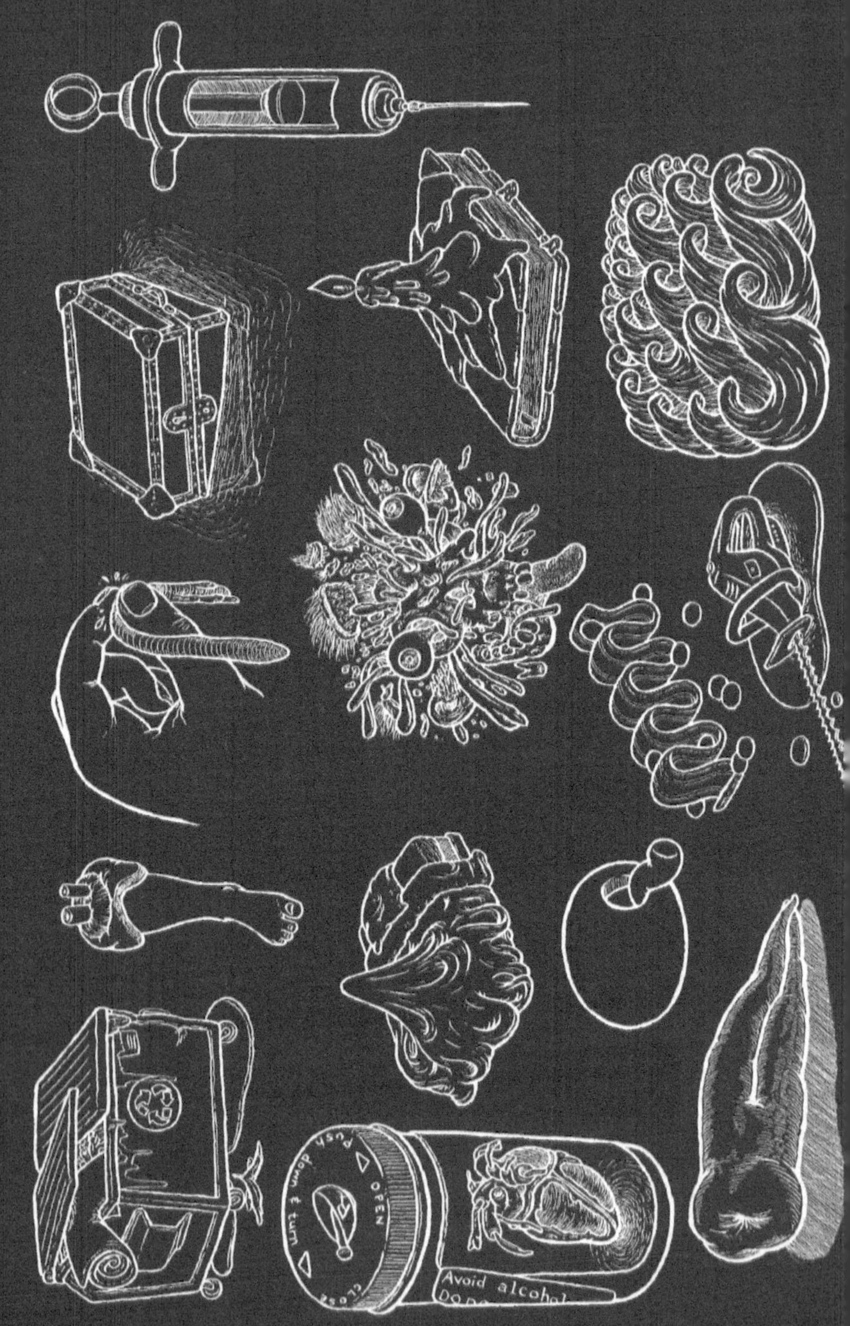
push down & turn
OPEN
close
Avoid alcohol

Gainesville

Gainesville

A Novel

Colin Winnette

Long Day Press
Chicago

Published by Long Day Press
Chicago, Il 60647
LongDayPress.com
@LongDayPress

ISBN 978-1-950987-47-4 (Paperback Edition)
ISBN 979-8-8693-2203-6 (eBook Edition)
Library of Congress Control Number: 2024937943

Cover and Layout by Joshua Bohnsack
Proofreading by Zoe Seipp

Images and cover interior art by Scott Teplin
https://teplin.com/

Previous edition published by Atticus Press in *Fondly*.
Excerpts published in *Housefire*.

Printed in the United States of America.
First Long Day Press Edition

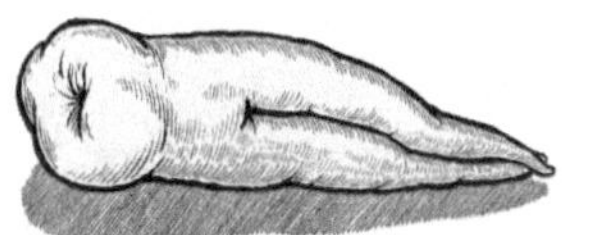

Foreword

Brian Evenson

A little over a decade ago, Colin Winnette emailed me out of the blue, saying that Lydia Millet, a writer I greatly admire, had recommended he reach out to me about reading and perhaps blurbing *Fondly*, a collection of two novellas. I was busy with teaching and also about a month away from the birth of my son Max, and so the chances that I'd be blurbing anything were slim at best, but I said, sure, go ahead, send it along. I opened the galley thinking I'd read a few pages and then send my apologies, but instead I found myself deeply engrossed—especially by one novella in particular, *Gainesville*, the work you find reprinted here. Once I started reading it, I found I couldn't stop.

What's so impressive to me about *Gainesville* is the way the story shifts its expectations. Initially it seems a straightforward piece of dirty realism set in Gainesville, Texas, focusing on a boy named Sonny. But just as you begin to settle into a certain comfort with that narrative, suddenly things change and Sonny is bundled (quite literally) out of the narrative. Indeed, Winnette deftly shifts the key he's playing in and reveals that what you thought was a country ballad about one hapless boy was in fact the overture for an intergenerational opera. The narrative gaze slides from Sonny to someone else (I won't reveal who, since the surprise of the shifts are part of the enjoyment) and then moves again, and again, and again. Soon you just have to hold on tight, waiting to see who and when Winnette will swerve to next.

George Saunders suggests in *A Swim in a Pond in the Rain* that "No worthy problem is ever solved within the plane of its original conception."[1] *Gainesville* strikes me as illustrating that notion admirably when it comes to the worthy problem of narrative form, and doing so in a distinctly contemporary way. The style of *Gainesville* is crisp and precise, the progression speedy. There's a Calvinoesque lightness to Winnette's writing here, in the way it seems to move from life to life like a stone skipping across the surface of a lake, touching down briefly and then taking off again. The narrative structure is clear and assured—but it's not the pattern you've come to expect from most fiction: instead of Freitag's looming pyramid it's like a scattering of sharpened caltrops. There's a mercilessness to it: a willingness on Winnette's part

---

1 Saunders attributes this quotation to Einstein, though as he himself admits, it may be more paraphrase than quotation.

to look unflinchingly at awfulness and not overtly judge it. Anything can happen to the characters here, and over the course of this brief, breathless book almost everything does. They are hapless, ground down by fate. Perhaps they are even cursed "for something that had happened so long ago no one could remember what it was, so they would remain cursed forever." And yet they also, somehow, persist, leaving a trail of damage behind. And, in the way that Winnette creates them, in the deft gestures and care of his language, they come fully, blazingly, painfully alive.

Gainesville is an original and compelling book that deserves a larger readership. It shows what narrative can do when it refuses to stick to the script, and it will stay with you long after you put the book down.

— Brian Evenson

It would be an exciting thing to see, all the cut trees stacked back and forth, and piled up toward the sky where there was only more space for them to be stacked higher. The boy, Sonny, took an axe to the first and looked around him thinking how easy it would be to just keep going, to axe this one then that one and never stop until all the trees were brought down and stacked and his arms were as big as cannons. He axed again and was a little more tired this time, but he thought of the cannons his arms would be and swung once more into the meat of the tree.

The axe stuck in the center of the trunk, so he had to pull just about as hard as he'd swung in order to remove the axe, and then he had to swing it again.

"If you stack them high enough," his brother said, "we can climb them and grip onto the edge of those rain clouds there and maybe slide over into the center of them."

Sonny knew his brother was probably lying, but he swung anyway. The idea was exciting.

Sonny's brother was sprawled out on the patio furniture, propped low in one swivel chair, with each extended leg rested on one of the two chairs in front of him. He was surrounded by beer bottles—some empty, some full. They were all warm.

Sonny's brother's friend, Rissa, was in the grass nearby. Sonny swung and looked back at Rissa and she pulled the grass out of the ground and stuck it in her shirt and Sonny thought about how great it would be if he were that grass sliding down and getting stuck.

Later they were all in the house and the axe was outside, leaned against the tree that was all marked up but still standing. They were watching TV, some show about teenagers trying things out, and Sonny asked Rissa if he could see where the grass had gone. She hit him in the mouth and told his brother and his brother hit him in the mouth a few times more and told him to get out so they could finish watching their show without the little pervert getting all worked up.

Sonny wandered around the house a few times before taking off down the road to the neighbor's house. He knocked on the door and the frog girl's mom answered and Sonny asked if Nicole was home and her mom went and got the frog girl. They called her the frog girl because her neck was as thick as her head and she gargled sometimes and spat, which they said was just like a frog, though it wasn't exactly.

The frog girl walked to the park with him, went on the swings with him, told him she liked the things he talked about—like cars and bicycles and his brother and his girlfriend—even though she didn't seem to be listening. Sonny got her to climb under the jungle gym by saying he'd found money there and when she was bent over, looking for the money, Sonny put his hand up her skirt and she started yelling and ran home to her mom, who definitely called Sonny's parents, so Sonny was scared to go home.

He walked a mile to the grocery store instead and pocketed a handful of beef jerky sticks and a beer from a six pack and tried to walk out with them, but the manager stopped him by tapping one shoulder and moving to the other side, so as to trick him. Sonny started to run, but the manager was faster. He got in between Sonny and the door.

"Call the police," said the manager, and Sonny started crying because the day had started out so well and all of a sudden it was the worst day ever. "Call the police," said the manager, "I've got him."

The police came and they arrested Sonny for stealing a beer and a handful of beef jerky sticks, and they brought him home to his parents who were upset with him already but were heartbroken and full of rage at the sight of him being unloaded from the police car.

Sonny's parents didn't know exactly how to handle a thing like this. Neither of them had misbehaved when growing up, not really, and they'd never gone beyond a grounding with Sonny's brother. But something severe had to happen, so Sonny's father took the boy into the living room and told him to drop his pants.

"My what?" Sonny said.

"Your pants and your underwear."

Sonny was convinced his father was joking until the man got irritated and tugged the boy's shorts down himself. Sonny started crying then and his father hit him a few times on the exposed skin, but the act didn't feel right, it only felt like a sloppy way of handling things, so he stopped after a few strikes. Sonny was sobbing and fell from his father's knee and just cried there in the middle of the room while the whole family watched and wondered what all of this might do. It didn't seem like it would do any good at all. Sonny's brother was happy to see the boy in trouble but didn't much like the sight of him crying and squirming in the middle of the room with his pants down.

Sonny was grounded for assaulting the neighbor girl and stealing a handful of beef jerky sticks and a beer. After a week or so, he snuck out to meet his friends at the junk pile in the woods behind most of the houses. Sonny's friend said he wanted to *B* and *E*, which was a way they could get money and Sonny said he would do it. The other boys said they wouldn't, that it seemed dangerous, and Sonny and his friend decided to *B* and *E* a neighbor's house so they could be quick about it. They chose Paul's house. Paul was a friend, but not a good friend. They'd been over enough times to know where things were and could easily get into the house, to all the good stuff, and out, before the cops could possibly get there.

They took the back way to Paul's house and checked the garage. Empty. So, they entered through the garage and snuck their way into the kitchen. They stole two beers each from the fridge. They hung them in their back pockets. Then they went into the bedroom and stole the condoms out of Paul's brother's drawer. They went into the bathroom and emptied the bottles in the cabinet into their pockets. They stuffed rags into the drains and turned on the water. They pulled a few books off the shelves. They went into the parents' bedroom and flipped through the CDs, found nothing, and started dropping the CD cases onto the ground. Sonny's friend knocked over a lamp. Sonny stepped on the lampshade. They pushed over a bookcase. Sonny took a set of earrings from a tiny box on the shelf, for Rissa.

They turned on the stove, turned on the oven. They opened the fridge and threw forks and spoons at the bottles of condiments inside. They got behind the fridge and pushed. It crashed to the ground and immediately began to leak. Brown and clear liquids seeped from the edges like from a wound. They knifed the couch pillows, turned on the fan and threw the cotton into the whirling blade. They took turns hitting the TV with an aluminum baseball bat. Sonny's friend jumped back after the blow and pretended to vibrate through and through. They could not stop laughing.

The police entered with their guns. Sonny and his friend went to a youth correctional facility in the heart of town, where they were held for six months each. Sonny wrote a letter to his parents and asked them to give it to Rissa and they did not, but they told him they did. Sonny's brother visited him one day and told him he was proud of him for doing the time and not getting into any trouble at the facility and that they were all excited for him to come home. Sonny said he was excited to come home too, because the facility was a terrible place and nobody treated him like a human being and he hated the cramped-up feelings he had all the time there, and why hadn't Mom and Dad come to visit him yet? Sonny's brother said they'd asked him to come and he'd agreed, but even he didn't like the idea of visiting Sonny out there in that place. When Sonny asked why, his brother said, "Because I hate thinking my brother deserves to be in a place like this."

Sonny didn't feel he deserved to be in a place like that. Looked at independently, the things he'd done hadn't been so bad, and he wasn't a bad person.

After six months, Sonny was released and so was his friend, but they hadn't talked much to one another in the facility and didn't plan on doing so now that they were out of it. Sonny's parents picked him up and they went out for French fries and ice cream to celebrate because he hadn't had ice cream in forever, and the French fries in the facility tasted like a sponge.

That night he slept in his own room in his very own bed. He started high school in two months, and he was going to get a whole new wardrobe and start living a little better than he had ever imagined.

The next week, it started raining. Sonny's family lived near the center of town, where the cheaper homes were, at low elevation. After only a few days of steady rain, they received the flood warning. They were asked to leave their homes until the rains passed. They did so, and watched the houses disintegrate and wash away on the TV in the hotel room.

They had insurance. Sonny's dad had the means to keep them comfortable in the meantime. He went to work, and the family started living out of room 227. Sonny and his brother slept on the floor, their parents in the full bed. They did this for two months.

Sonny tried meth with his brother. They both liked it. They liked it a lot. They asked their parents for money and were given it occasionally. They spent the money almost entirely on drugs. Sonny's brother had patience. He was like a Buddhist, Sonny said. Sonny started calling him Buddha. Not only because he'd put on a good deal of weight since they left their home, but also because he was remarkably in control of his cravings. When they were low on money, Sonny's brother could wait and wait, until their parents dished out a little more. Sonny would go crazy each time, not knowing when they would get more money, not knowing where, if they did, they would be able to get quality drugs. Sonny called his older brother Buddha until his older brother hit him in the mouth one afternoon while their parents were out. Sonny's brother hit him over and over again and Sonny collapsed and took the beating like a log. Sonny didn't get up. Sonny's brother rolled him over.

Sonny's brother wrapped Sonny in the hotel comforter. He stepped out of the room, looked both ways, then dragged the comforter out and down the hallway toward the stairs. He dragged it down the stairs, through the thump after thump, then to the fire exit. The door said an alarm would sound, but Sonny's brother knew it wouldn't. They'd used the exit a number of times before. The first time, Sonny had looked at the sign, then at his brother, and said, "Fuck it."

Sonny's brother dragged the comforter into the alley behind the building. He folded it, lifted it, and slid it into the dumpster. It hit the bottom like a cabbage.

Sonny's brother went back to the hotel room. There was a little blood on the carpet. He scrubbed it with one of the hotel towels and a bit of two-in-one shampoo plus conditioner. The stain lifted and he threw the towel away and phoned the front desk to request another comforter.

"For the boys," he said.

When his parents came home, Sonny's brother explained that Sonny had gone out hours before and hadn't returned.

"He had that look in his eye," Sonny's brother said.

His father nodded, though this was not an expression they'd used before in reference to anything.

Sonny's parents were up through the night waiting for him to come home, for a phone call, for anything. But nothing came.

In the morning, Sonny's father called the police. The garbage man made his rounds, stopping at each dumpster in the alley. He complained at how full they were, and Sonny's dad plugged his ears to quiet the sound of the truck and the garbage men yelling.

Sonny became a missing person. Sonny's brother got a job as the night manager at a Kmart. He partnered up with one of the cashiers. She had a gold tooth, but never wore jewelry. She was soft spoken. She straightened her hair with an iron. She was either slow or shy, or both, Sonny's brother couldn't tell, but she liked him. She started following him to his car.

They had a baby and got a place together on the edge of town. Sonny's brother was a hard worker; he was promoted within three months. His girlfriend hated the work, said it was exhausting. She'd already cut her hours back to take care of the baby, so he encouraged her to quit.

"The baby," he said.

They named the baby James, but Sonny's brother called the baby Rickets.

"Like Jiminy Cricket," he explained, but she still didn't like it.

When the baby was two, Sonny's brother was put in charge of a store. He had night terrors. He developed Bruxism. He was very polite at work.

His girlfriend let the baby sunburn in the parking lot while she haggled over the price of a T-shirt at a street fair.

"The guy was being unreasonable," she said, and Sonny's brother tore an abstract poster from the wall. He threw a lamp, not at anyone, but at the ground by his feet. The baby was crying from the noise and from rolling onto the burns and Sonny's brother said his girlfriend was a bitch, a bitch, a bitch and that he was taking the baby and that he was leaving and good luck to her with the rest of it.

In the morning, he packed and left for work. When he got home, she'd packed the baby's things. He took the things, rented a hotel room. He stopped calling the baby Rickets and started calling the baby Sonny.

Sonny's brother rented a duplex near the Kmart he was responsible for. He applied for a loan so he could start a small business, but he was declined. Sonny's brother started drinking. He thought about the drugs he used to like to do. Sonny was three.

Sonny's brother called the baby both Jiminy and Sonny. He wrote Sonny (Jiminy) on a preschool application. The teachers were excited to have a redhead. They had no other redheads. Jiminy was an adorable redhead.

Sonny's brother got letters in the mail from his ex-girlfriend asking after Rickets and Sonny's brother wrote back, *I don't call him Rickets anymore.*

Jiminy loved school. He loved playing with the other kids. When he was old enough, he started telling stories all the time to anyone who would listen. He told stories about things he'd heard other people talk about and filled in what he didn't know.

"My dad pays the electricity to a man who wants him to pay every month because that man also has to pay electricity every month but has to pay more for his electricity because he owns the machine that pumps electricity and that uses even more electricity than the machines we use in our house."

Sonny's brother wrote Jiminy's stories down and sometimes put them on the refrigerator.

"Sonny," he said, "You're a great storyteller."

Sonny's brother and Jiminy went to the park almost every day.

Sonny's brother liked to watch him play and use the slide and talk to the other kids. That was something Sonny's brother had never been good at, talking to other kids, other people. He'd kept to himself most of his life, and, watching Sonny, he began to realize that he didn't like that feeling. He didn't like being surrounded by people he couldn't connect with.

"How old is yours?" he asked a woman who was sitting at the center of a bench near the swings.

"Five," she answered. She didn't move.

He sat down beside her.

"Nearly four," he said. He pointed to Jiminy at the top of the slide.

"Is your wife a redhead?"

"Girlfriend," he said, "was a redhead… or she *is* a redhead… *was* my girlfriend."

The woman made a sound like, *oh*.

"What about you?" he asked. "Your wife a redhead?" She

laughed. Her husband was.

"How long have you been married?" he asked.

"Six years—honey!"

Her daughter held a woodchip between her front teeth. She was digging for more.

"Honey, take that out of your mouth."

"He's a lucky…"

"Excuse me," she said.

That night, Sonny's brother watched Jiminy eat and thought about how terribly alone he was. Jiminy pressed his palm into a pile of peas.

Sonny's brother pulled out his computer and entered his information into the entry form for an online dating program. He was a single father, 6'2", 185 lb., white. He didn't like partying. He loved his son. He was interested in anything available but wasn't desperate for a relationship. He liked music.

In the morning, he fed Jiminy. He turned on the TV and gave the boy his nebulizer. Jiminy needed fifteen minutes on the thing each morning. Jiminy watched TV and held up his nebulizer and made little noises while Sonny's brother checked his email and found three responses to his post. He wrote the same message to all three women:

You sound like a really interesting person. I'd love to meet up sometime, maybe just on the phone. Here's my number. Call whenever you like. If I'm at work, leave a message. I look forward to it.

He dropped Jiminy off at school and came home to find one voicemail from a woman named Clara. Clara wanted to talk on the phone, so Sonny's brother called her and they spoke for nearly an hour. Clara also worked in retail; she was a saleswoman at Best Buy. And, yes, she had all kinds of neat home entertainment equipment as a result. Sonny's brother said he wasn't that concerned with home entertainment; his hands were full when he was at home. But he got some time away, every now and then, and he was grateful for it.

"Would you have time this weekend?" Clara asked.

He would.

Sonny's brother arranged for a sitter. He called Jiminy's school for a recommendation and they put him in touch with Kids Plus, a local service. They arranged for a sitter to arrive at four and stay until seven that night.

The sitter showed up in cutoffs and a tank top and Sonny's brother thought she couldn't have been over nineteen. She was chewing gum and as she walked through the doorway she asked if there were any songs Jiminy liked or anything like that.

"Any songs?" said Sonny's brother.

When she bent over to pick up Jiminy, Sonny's brother saw the edge of her ass dip beneath the fray of her shorts.

"I don't know," he said. "Not really. 'Puff the Magic Dragon,'" he lied.

"Really?" she asked. "That's such a sad song."

Clara was a little overweight. She'd lied on the form. It didn't matter. She liked coffee, so they went for coffee.

"You were able to get a sitter?" she asked.

"Yeah, you should have… she was very young. I don't know what they're thinking," he said, "sending such young women as sitters."

"I used to babysit when I was young," she said. "Women have a preternatural knack for that kind of thing. He'll be fine, I'm sure."

"How long does it take to pour two goddamn cups of coffee?" Sonny's brother said. He laughed. He bit his nails, the pointer first, then the thumb, on each hand. He spit them into his palm, lowered his hand to his side, and dropped them on the ground.

"Do you like working at Kmart?"

He didn't. But he was good at it. It was easy work. You just had to follow the rules. You had to be firm. You had to keep an eye on everything at all times. You had to be on top of everything and everyone, always.

"Yes."

The coffees arrived.

"Sorry," he said. "I'm a little nervous."

"It's cute," she said.

This, he thought, *is going well.*

After coffee, she asked him over. They sat on her couch, and she put on music. She offered him wine.

"You just move through the day," he said, "tweaking your high?"

She laughed. She touched his knee. There was something charming about him, she said. He was sweet and nervous, and she liked that. Most of the guys she met online were creeps. He wasn't a creep. She kissed him on the neck. It had been a long time since he'd felt a thing like that. He kissed her on the neck. She told him she knew she wanted to kiss him from the moment he'd walked into the coffee shop.

"How?" he said.

"How what?"

"How did you know?"

She leaned back and took a sip of her wine. She opened a window.

"I don't know," she said. "Maybe I didn't know. But I wanted to."

It was 6:45. He had to go. He didn't know what happened if you were late for a babysitter. He told her as much, and she said he could call. They might charge extra, but he could call. He said he would see her again, maybe later that week, and she agreed. He left her alone with the wine and the open window and he ran down to the car and called himself *stupid, stupid, stupid*, until he was finally home and walking through the door and announcing himself to the babysitter and Jiminy, who were curled up on the couch together, sleeping to a commercial for two double cheeseburgers.

Sonny's brother called Clara the next morning and she didn't answer. He called her again in the afternoon and got nothing. He waited two days. He called her again and when she didn't answer he left a message asking how she was, how she'd been. He'd love to see her again, he said. No pressure.

Nothing.

A week later, he called for a sitter.

"The redhead," he said. "My kid's a redhead."

She arrived, sans gum, and said, "'Puff the Magic Dragon,' right?"

Sonny's brother drove to Clara's house and saw the lights were on and so he knocked and when she came to the door, she couldn't have looked more annoyed.

"What?"

"I called you," he said.

"I know," she said. "I've… I've been busy."

"We had a nice time," he said.

"And you left," she said.

"I have a kid."

"You could have called and had the sitter stay a little longer," she said. "I used to be a babysitter and I know you could have, but you didn't want to."

"So you've been ignoring my calls?"

"Yes."

He left.

When he arrived home, he found the sitter and Jiminy sitting on the floor in the living room, an entire box of Legos splayed between the sitter's two widespread legs. Jiminy was at her feet, pressing the blocks together.

"Will you have sex with me for money?" Sonny's brother said.

The babysitter looked up. Jiminy looked up.

"For how much?" she asked.

Sonny's brother used Kids Plus once a week. Then twice a week. At first, "The redhead." Then, "Jen."

"I don't do this with anybody else," she explained. It didn't matter.

Not really. That's what he liked about it. Her time was her time. For a few hours a week, she was on *their* time. As long as she wasn't doing it with other men while she was on *their* time, it didn't matter.

"It doesn't matter," he said.

"One time, Dad was at work and someone told him she was going to call his supervisor because Dad is an overemotional worker and then Dad was worried for a long time because what if she did that?, and he thought he was going to get fired and then he didn't get fired."

"Is that true," she asked. "Are you an overemotional worker?"

"Sometimes," he said. "I guess I am."

"Like when?"

“Dad turned off the gas one time because fuck the gas company and…”

“Jiminy,” Sonny’s brother said, “language.”

“And—sorry—and they didn’t turn off the gas, so we got free gas for a month and then he started paying again.”

“That’s nice of you,” she said. “Can I smoke in here?”

“No,” Sonny’s brother said.

“Then I’ve got to go.”

“You should stay,” said Sonny’s brother.

“Can’t smoke in here,” she said.

Sonny’s brother made the babysitter leave the door open when she used the bathroom, for whatever reason. He didn’t know her that well. He left it at that.

“What are you doing tomorrow?” she asked from the shower.

"Why?" he asked. He was prone, in bed.

"Don't get all freaked out," she said, "Kids Plus is having a customer picnic. Looking to recruit some new folks and feed some regulars."

"You want me there to boast the lengths you'll go to keep the kids happy?"

"I just meant to say there'd be free food there, and free drinks, and lots of kids for Jiminy to meet and you don't have to be a shithead."

The shower shut off and she entered the bedroom in a yellow towel. He tugged at the towel's edge.

"What have you got under there?"

"He's a good kid, and he likes people," she said.

"I don't know where he gets it from."

He began to kiss her neck.

"Have you thought about starting a family?"

He pulled the towel away.

"A wife? Another kid?"

"Yeah," he said, "that's good. Keep it up. Ask me about life insurance."

He pulled her down to the bed, laid her on her back. He kissed her stomach, her neck, her ears. He ran his hands along the side of her head and moved down, kissing as he went.

"Jiminy could use a sibling, maybe. A sister," she said. He lightly thumbed her throat. "Or a brother."

He kissed her between her legs. She whispered something. He pinched her nipple. He took his time, though the clock was running. She came and he pulled back, he hit her once across the face. Then again. He hit her again, in the chest. She started screaming.

She screamed, "What the fuck?" and he hit her again. He hit her again and again and again and she reached beside her and grabbed the lamp and threw it at him, as hard as she could. It didn't break, but it hit his arm and chest hard and fell onto the bed. She sat up and lifted the lamp with both hands and hit him in the face, on the back of the head, and again. He fell into the bed, face first and she hit him again and again and again until he rose up and batted the lamp away. She leapt from the bed, darted to the door.

"You motherfucker," she said.

Jiminy said, "Dad?" from the other room.

"You piece of shit," she said.

He was breathing hard, bleeding and breathing and hunched over on the bed. She backed up toward the door then paused. She picked up an aluminum baseball bat from where it was propped against the bookcase. She swung once, landed the blow on the side of his head.

"You piece of shit."

She swung again. She swung until her arms went limp and Jiminy was pushing the door open. She pushed the door back.

"Just a second sweetie," she said.

"Dad?"

"He's sleeping," she said. "Just a second."

Jiminy was less social in grade school. He didn't seem interested in girls. He did well on the tests, on his homework. He didn't like to talk in the halls. During recess, he swung his arms. He moved around underneath the monkey bars and swung his arms and made smashing sounds. He went to a small school. The other kids were nice enough. Most of them, anyway. But he avoided them. He was quiet in class too, didn't take well to being called on, asked for an answer. Every now and then, he cried. The teachers brought his foster parents in, told them their son was having trouble *fitting in.* He was exhibiting an unhealthy level of reticence. Jiminy's foster parents were grateful for the notice. They'd asked to be alerted as to his social adjustments. They were worried for him, not about him.

"Jim," they said. "We'd like to invite some of your friends over this weekend."

He didn't want them to.

"We think it would be nice to have a few friends over, Jim."

"No," he said.

"Just a few," said his foster mother.

She made the calls. Jiminy cried in his bedroom. His foster father stood outside the door.

"Son," he said. "Your mother and I think it will be good for you to see your friends outside of school. You'll be able to have more fun."

"I don't have any friends," Jiminy said.

"Some of your classmates, then," said his foster father, "who will become your friends."

"The Millers can't," said Jiminy's foster mother, "But the Jones boy is coming and… Susie Parker."

"Hear that?"

Nothing.

That weekend Susie Parker and Sam Jones came over to Jiminy's new house. The three of them sat in the patio furniture and ate chips and Sam asked,

"What's that?" He pointed to Jiminy's treehouse.

Jiminy shrugged.

"It's a treehouse," Susie said. "Can we climb it?"

Jiminy shrugged again. He crumbled a chip in his hand, scattered the flakes onto the table.

"Mr. Legit, can we climb the tree house?" Sam said.

"Of course," said Jiminy's foster father.

"I'll have to show you how," Jiminy said.

Underneath the tree house, Jiminy loosed a rope from between two low branches of a nearby tree. He threw the rope up, knocked down the stepladder, which came down swinging. They each took a step back, and Jiminy reached out, grabbed the ladder and began to climb.

Susie and Sam followed.

The treehouse was dark inside, shaded. There were milk crates to sit on, books to read. There was a board game, Monopoly, missing all of the money and most of the pieces.

"What do you do up here?" asked Susie.

"I think about you," Jiminy said.

Susie blushed. She touched a bow on her sock. Sam Jones laughed.

"That's not all he does," he said.

Jiminy looked at Sam and said, "You can leave."

"I don't want to leave," said Sam Jones.

"Then you have to be nicer."

That evening, Jiminy's foster mother lit some citronella candles and they all gathered around the picnic table and ate brisket and macaroni and mashed potatoes and coleslaw and watched the fireflies stir as the sun went down.

"Can we go to the haunted van?" Jiminy asked.

His foster mother paused. She looked at her son, looked him in the eyes, and Jiminy shifted in his seat.

"Next time, Sonny."

"The haunted van?" Susie asked.

"Next time," Jiminy said.

"When is next time?" asked Sam Jones.

"We'll have to talk with your parents, but next weekend?" Jiminy's foster mother said. "Sunday is family day and homework day. And Jiminy does his studies during the week."

"How about next Saturday?" said Jiminy.

His foster parents stood by the grill together.

"That's just fine," said his foster father.

The next weekend, Sam Jones and Susie Parker came over to investigate the haunted van. Jiminy led them out the back door and into a field. They pulled apart the wire of a barbed-wire fence and climbed through to the other side. They wandered, as the grass grew taller. They walked for nearly half an hour before Susie asked,

"How much further?"

"Not much," said Jiminy, "It's just right around here somewhere."

They reached a creek. They went down to the creek's edge. It was narrow enough to cross, but they were going to get wet.

"You have to cross," said Jiminy.

Sam started walking. He stepped into the water and kept on until he was calf deep.

"I don't want to," Susie said.

Sam and Jiminy shrugged.

"Stay right there, then," Jiminy said.

Sam and Jiminy crossed the creek. They walked up the creek bed and climbed over the edge. There were woods ahead of them, and taller grass. They walked on. They walked for nearly fifteen minutes before Jiminy said,

"There is no haunted van."

"Okay," said Sam. "Then what are we even doing out here?"

"I don't know," said Jiminy. "Are you mad?"

"No," said Sam. "Liar."

"Can we scare Susie and tell her we saw ghosts?" asked Jiminy.

Sam said, "Yes."

The two of them ran back toward the creek, they bolted across the water, caught Susie off guard, and told her to run, run for her life, run as fast as she could. The three of them darted back across the field. Sam and Jiminy screamed at the top of their lungs. Susie began to scream too. She began to cry. She kept running. They climbed through the barbed-wire fence. Susie was breathing heavy, she was screaming and crying and the boys were screaming and holding back laughter and they all ran into Jiminy's foster parents' house and collapsed into the living room. They screamed from their collapsed positions and Sam and Jiminy rolled around while Susie lay on her stomach screaming into the carpet. Jiminy's foster father appeared in the living room asking,

"What's wrong? What's wrong? What's happened?" over and over again until Jiminy stopped screaming and said nothing was wrong, they were just playing.

"What's wrong with her?" asked Jiminy's foster father.

Susie was crying and curled up and covering her head.

"What happened, Sonny?"

"Nothing happened, Dad, we just scared her a little."

"We were just playing, Mr. Legit, honest."

"Susie," said Jiminy's foster father. "Susie, hon, what's wrong?"

She wouldn't uncurl.

"We were just playing," said Sam.

Sam and Jiminy went into middle school together and then high school. They started drinking together and traded porn until Sam had sex, then kept having sex, and Jiminy was left to his own devices. When they were seniors, they got tattoos. They did well in high school. They did what they wanted, for the most part. Sam was popular and Jiminy was Sam's friend. Sam played baseball and had late night baseball parties. Jiminy hit on his baseball friends. Jiminy let the varsity pitcher fuck him on the washing machine at Sam's house. The pitcher's girlfriend found out about it and painted *homo* on Jiminy's car in pink spray paint. Jiminy outlined it in gold.

"You're gay?" asked his foster father.

"I think so," he said.

"Your mother's not going to like it."

"She'll get over it."

Jiminy got the pitcher's number from Sam. Sam was reluctant, told Jiminy to let it go, but Jiminy insisted. He called the pitcher at all hours of the night until finally the pitcher told him to meet him where Collins Road met Fair, just outside of town. Jiminy brought an aluminum baseball bat.

The pitcher was there, sitting on the roof of his car when Jiminy arrived. "You've got to stop calling me," said the pitcher.

"Start answering," said Jiminy.

"I'm already in enough trouble as it is," said the pitcher. "Just leave me alone, okay?"

"You want me to leave you alone?"

"I'm asking you to leave me alone," said the pitcher.

Jiminy thought about the baseball bat. He thought about the washer, the spray paint, Sam.

"Fine," he said.

Jiminy bought opium for the first time from an Irish guy at a Mexican bar.

"How do I know it's real?" he asked.

"Smell it," said the Irish guy, "smoke it. It's real." He pocketed the money.

Jiminy smoked opium on the roof of a used bookstore in the middle of downtown. He felt sleepy, but not tired. Things seemed a little easier. He thought he saw the pitcher's truck. It didn't matter. He was on the roof. He thought he saw a shooting star. He wasn't sure. There was an ant on the back of his hand.

In the morning, he would take better notes. He would become a straight A student, because, what the fuck, why not? Everything else was shitty, why not kick ass in school and let everyone go fuck them selves?

He took better notes. He did a little better. Not a lot, but a little. He smoked opium on the roofs of old buildings, anything with a fire escape. Sam came a few times, said he didn't like it. It didn't do anything, really. Just slowed him down. Sam was into activity now. Jiminy preferred to relax. He aced a few tests.

His parents were proud. He was in love with opium.

When the Irish guy disappeared, Jiminy bought oxycodone from a friend of Sam's. That knocked him on his ass. He couldn't take much of it at all. Sometimes he threw up. Other times, he passed out, or fell.

Jiminy's foster father had a heart attack. They visited him in the hospital and Jiminy pocketed some of his heart medication. He took it with a beer. He took great notes. Aced another test. He took the heart medication with a glass of absinthe.

"It's real," Sam swore. "It's imported."

They both took the heart medication. They got drunk on absinthe, forewent the ritual and drank it straight from the bottle.

Jiminy kissed Sam and Sam kissed him back for a second. Then he stopped.

Jiminy took more of the heart medication and Sam drank more of the absinthe.

Sam copied Jiminy's answers on an English test and they both aced the test together.

They graduated from high school and went to a number of parties afterward. They were both drunk and driving from one end of town to the other. They filled the car with girls Sam was interested in. Jiminy was rude to all of them. He started crying halfway through the night and locked himself in the bathroom at one of the parties. He took all of the oxycodone he had and passed out. He woke up in the emergency room, passed out again. He woke up strapped to a bed. He passed out again.

He was in a facility because he'd tried to kill himself. He hadn't actually, but that's what they told him.

His foster mother came to visit. She looked like a ghost. She didn't look real. She told him his room was exactly how he'd left it. There was food waiting for him when he got home. She was happy to see him with a little color in his cheeks. She started crying. She always cried. He told her he didn't mean to kill himself and that made her cry even harder.

Sam came to visit and said Jiminy needed to curb his drinking.

"I'm worried about you."

Sam went to college out of state. He played baseball until he hurt his shoulder. Then he coached. He had three daughters.

Jiminy and Sam talked on the phone once a month or so. Jiminy got a job cleaning pools. He could smoke while he worked, show up drunk from the night before, if necessary. Jiminy liked an easy job. Sam wanted a hard job, and it broke him. Neither of them was what they had expected, but they didn't know what they had expected.

Jiminy got a girlfriend with a dead tooth. She laughed all the time, at almost everything he said. And he liked that most of the time. He liked saying something and her laughing and feeling good about himself even when he didn't know the best thing to say. She also liked to party. So, they drank a lot and screwed a lot and things were good in that way. She screwed around too but it didn't matter because Jiminy always imagined that he would screw around too, as soon as he met the right guy. It was easier being with a girl who laughed all the time.

"Sounds like a winner," Sam said.

"Fuck you," said Jiminy. "Are we even friends anymore?"

Jiminy broke into the morgue and stole a jar of formaldehyde and started dipping his cigarettes in it. He had dreams that he was swimming and woke up on the job in the customer's pool, as they were pulling in from wherever they'd been. He climbed out, he'd slipped. He was awful sorry about it. The customer shook his head and carried the brown paper bag full of groceries into the house. He called to cancel the regular service and when Jiminy was asked why, he said he couldn't understand it.

"He said you were swimming in his pool," said Raul, owner of Deep Blue.

"Well, I wasn't," said Jiminy.

Jiminy was put on probation at work and he resented it and started staying up later than usual and trying to say mean things to his girlfriend so she wouldn't laugh, but she laughed anyway, most of the time, until she finally said, "You don't want me around, do you?" and he knew exactly what he could say back, the one thing she couldn't possibly laugh at, and he said, "No, I don't," and she started laughing and laughing while she packed and spilled her drink and laughed some more and left.

A couple of weeks later she came back to their old apartment and knocked and no one answered, so she used her old keys to let herself in, and she discovered Jiminy slumped in the center of the room, nearly two weeks dead. The phone was ringing. She picked it up to dial 911 and Raul was on the other end. There was a problem with Jiminy's last paycheck. He hadn't signed the timesheet, and they couldn't pay him until he did.

"Jiminy's dead," said his ex-girlfriend, "I think. But I need the paycheck. I'm pregnant."

Raul said she would have to come in.

"What happened to you?" asked Raul. "You used to be so lighthearted, and you're so serious. So sad."

"I'm pregnant," she said. "And I come home to find the father dead in the living room."

"It's sad, yes," said Raul. "But maybe Jiminy would not have been the best role model? Maybe he could have pulled things together, yes. But who knows? You are a very beautiful woman. You will find another man to love you and take care of you and you don't need to be so sad. Life is very good."

“I’m broke,” she said.

“You’ll come work for me,” he said.

“Really?”

“You’ll be a secretary and coordinator. You’ll organize the schedules, assign my boys jobs they can work in succession. One after the other, huh? Less driving around, wasting time. You’ve done this kind of thing before?”

“Of course,” she lied. She laughed when they shook hands. He smiled.

Raul brought her gifts throughout the day. Chocolates, jewelry found in public pools. He told her she was doing a great job. She started to show after three months. After six, people began to say she was *full blown pregnant.*

She was great at her job. She had a knack for working Raul’s boys to the bone. For the most part they liked taking orders from her. They liked how clean her plans were. She organized things by neighborhood and by the type of job request.

Cleaners went out in a caravan, and the de-cloggers went on specialty missions, house by house. There was no overlap, and no crew had to switch gear. She was an expert.

Raul admired her hair, her dress. He gave her a raise and said it was for work wear. He thought she deserved to look more professional. She bought a pair of shoes. While she leaned over to drink at the water fountain, he placed his hand on the small of her back. She rose into it. Neither of them said anything.

At eight months, she went on leave. Raul came to visit her at home. He brought her items she needed from the store when she wasn't up to it. He rubbed her feet while she pried open a jar of mayonnaise.

They watched television together when he was tired from a day at work without her and she was lonely from day after day of being by herself in Jiminy's old apartment. Raul was there when the baby was born.

He drove her home. He was enthralled, had never seen anything like it.

"You were so strong," he said.

She was busy with the baby, just watching it. That thing had come out of her. That little thing, moving around and looking at nothing in particular. It seemed strange to hold it. She'd held it so well the months before, and now it was in her hands and making her nervous. Raul paced in front of them. He wanted to see more. He wanted to be a doctor, be a nurse on the maternity ward, be a gynecologist, be a dad. He got down on one knee.

"Will you marry me?" he asked.

She lifted her arms, settled the baby's head against her upper arm. The thing kept shifting, readjusting, so she had to shift and readjust as well. She couldn't get entirely comfortable. She was nervous about the thing's fragility. The baby coughed and foam came out.

"Yes," she said. She wiped the foam away with her sleeve.

They moved in together. She stayed on maternity leave and worked a little from home. Raul brought her the schedules and she coordinated things in her off hours, which were few. He watched the baby and sent her to the dentist. He fixed her dead tooth. She didn't laugh like she used to, but things were better than they'd ever been. She was safe. She had a home.

She had a family. She missed the casual fun of a guy like Jiminy. She missed the danger, too. She missed fighting. She and Raul never fought. Even when she pushed him—nothing.

They had more children: two girls and another boy. The children all had dark skin, like their father. Jiminy's son, Osiris, was a pale red head. The two girls grew up the best of friends. Osiris and his brother, Michael, did not get along. They fought over toys. They fought over food. They fought over space on the carpet.

"That is what boys do," said Raul.

"It's not all they do," insisted Jiminy's ex-girlfriend.

Michael was two years younger than Osiris, but twice his size. At three, Michael sat on Osiris's arm in the backyard and broke two of his fingers. Michael did not want to tell his parents and Osiris cried and cried while Michael pretended to play in the grass. Eventually Raul came home from work and found Osiris crying, his hand swollen like a ripe fruit, and he rushed him to the hospital. Raul spanked Michael. Raul was a big fan of spanking. He spanked Michael until Michael was through crying. Raul asked Michael, over and over again, between spankings, if he knew why this was happening, and

Michael said, yes, because he'd hurt Osiris, and Raul said, "Yes, you hurt him very badly."

Michael and Osiris grew up at odds. Michael went to a private school, Osiris to a specialty school. He was slower than the other kids. He had trouble holding on to an idea, trouble forming sentences, trouble speaking in public. He was diagnosed with mild autism, dyslexia. He wore glasses and had a stutter. Raul was a very kind father to him. He patted the boy on the head when they were at the table. He held him in his lap while they watched movies or TV.

Michael told his mother he felt lonely. He did not think his dad loved him as much as Osiris.

"Your father loves you both," she said, "equally."

She was in bed when she said it. She spent most of the day in bed. She took pills from a series of jars at the bedside. She had trouble standing up, trouble walking. There was something off in her hips. Raul waited on her hand and foot. He also worked overtime with the kids. He brought them to school, picked them up. He made dinner for the family and made sure to spend some time with them between homework and lights out. She admired Raul. She admired his determination, his strength. She did not want to go back to work. The idea of more scheduling and rescheduling was appalling.

"You don't have to work," said Raul. "But you do need to help with the house, with the children. You cannot sleep late all the time and shut yourself away. It's not fair to me or to them."

"Your father picks favorites," she later told Michael. "You must have done something to upset him."

Michael remembered the spanking, Osiris's hand. He was extra nice to his sisters. He played with them even when he didn't want to.

One afternoon, Michael helped them dig a hole in the backyard and fill it with water from the hose attached to the back of the house. They dug the hole a few feet deep with a shovel they'd found in the garage.

"Goddammit," said Raul when he got home from work. "Look what you've done."

He found his wife in the bed, asleep.

"Have you seen what your children did to the lawn?" he asked.

She stirred, rolled, drew a pillow between her knees.

"No."

"They are destroying the lawn," he said. "They have destroyed the lawn."

"And you worked so hard on that lawn," she said.

"Don't talk shit to me. I worked very hard on the lawn. I want us to have a respectable house, to be a respectable family. I do not want us to live in filth and have filthy things. We do not need that, and I won't have it." He went outside and yelled for the children to get out of the hole, to rinse off. He would bring them towels. This was not right, he explained. They were doing harm.

They were laughing and covered in mud and beautiful to look at, he realized. They were grounded, he told them. One week each. Everyone except for Osiris, who had been in the house for most of it, though he had helped start the hole earlier that afternoon.

That night, Michael punched Osiris in the nose while he was sleeping. Osiris started bleeding and yelling and crying and Raul burst into the bedroom and grabbed Michael by both shoulders, lifted him, carried him into the living room where he yanked down the boy's shorts and spanked him and spanked him and spanked him. Michael was a sobbing, snotty mess in the center of the room when Raul left. He dabbed peroxide on Osiris's nose. He stuffed the bleeding hole with toilet paper. He came back out into the living room to find Michael sitting upright, leaned against the wall.

"I hate you," Michael said. "I want to kill you."

Raul went into the kitchen. He poured himself a drink and sat at the table. The boy did not want to kill him, he told himself. He poured himself another drink. The boy could not kill him if he tried.

Raul climbed into bed beside his wife.

"What is wrong?" he asked.

That made her curl tighter.

“How are you?” he tried.

“I’m fine,” she said, and curled.

“What can I do for you?” he said. “You seem unhappy.”

“I am unhappy,” she said.

“What can I do for you?”

“. . .”

“What can I do for you, my love?”

“Not everything is about you.”

She was alone in her room most of the time. She cut her fingernails short. Too short. She pulled on the ends of her hair until strands came loose between her fingers. She thought, *Maybe I should go to a doctor*, and took handful after handful of Tylenol, Advil, ibuprofen. What was wrong with her? She didn’t like to think about it. Maybe Jiminy had gotten her sick. Maybe he was a deeply disturbed person and that had infected her somehow. During the day, when her kids were at school and her husband was at work, she felt almost at peace. But the moment they all arrived home, the house was in an uproar and the noise did not stop until late in the night when it was replaced by the sound of Raul flipping through channel after channel until he fell asleep. This was not what she'd expected from her life.

She sued Raul for custody of their four kids, and she won. She told her lawyer that Raul struck the children, he played favorites, he did not get enough sleep, and he was often cruel to her and the others. Michael testified that Raul had indeed struck him. Osiris was very overwhelmed by the witness stand, the court proceedings. He wept openly before the judge, his parents, the court. The two daughters both said that they loved their parents. Their mom and their dad. They loved them.

She kept Jiminy's apartment. Raul wasn't allowed within one hundred feet.

Outside of the courtroom he called her a snake and a bitch and said she would not get away with it. He said she would murder their children. He said this was a death sentence.

But the truth was, she was much happier without him around.

She woke up with the kids, took them to school. She received checks from Raul, checks from the government, and she was able to feed the children and herself, to keep them clothed. At home, she cleaned from time to time. She learned how to darn socks, how to fix a hem.

Raul sent letters with the checks, asked how the kids were, how Osiris was adjusting to middle school. She didn't write back.

Raul went back to cleaning pools. He spent less and less time managing the place, and more and more time out on jobs. He went alone. He spent hours on a single job. His boys started taking their time too. Raul was gone all the time, so they felt less pressure to perform. Deep Blue lost business. Raul cleaned and smoked cigarettes. He skimmed the pools over and over again with a bluish net at the end of a long handle. He walked slowly along the edge of the pool then back again, delicately.

Raul pounded on Jiminy's old apartment door. It was nearly midnight. The TV was on at high volume. Raul pounded and yelled and wanted his kids back and his life back and his ex-wife didn't answer but turned up the TV instead. He saw Michael in the window, and he waved to him. Michael disappeared.

Raul went home. Raul enlisted in the army. He went to training camp only two months later. He slept better than he had in years. He woke up early. He worked out. He learned about a variety of weapons. He ate the minimum amount. Lost weight, gained very little muscle. Deep Blue was in the hands of his top guy, Joe. Joe did fine, kept the company afloat. Raul went to war.

Raul was the gunner in the second Humvee in a caravan. One morning, they came across what appeared to be an abandoned village. Their translator announced their presence. He warned the occupants to come out, unarmed. No one responded. They fired warning shots into the dirt by one of the larger buildings on the town's perimeter. Nothing. The caravan entered the village.

Osiris's mom made him an apple pie from scratch for his birthday. She worked in the kitchen all the time now. She was always trying things out. She brought friends over two or three nights a week. They tried drink recipes from magazines. They tried different fruits and vegetables in different shapes, pressed against different parts of their bodies. Cucumber slivers over their eyes, carrot skins down the length of their arms and legs. They rubbed avocado into their palms and over their hands. They drank pink drinks and purple drinks and brown drinks with clear drinks dropped into them. Several of her friends came to Osiris's birthday party. They had a special punch in a bowl on the counter. Osiris ate three slices of pie. Michael had one. His sisters none. One sister had fattened up, while the other had grown very skinny. His fat sister was moody but laughed a lot like his mother. His skinny sister was very shy at home, but extremely popular in school. The skinny sister did not like to be around food. The fat sister did not like to be around people and food. She took a slice of pizza to her bedroom. The skinny sister asked to have some of the punch and her mother poured her a very small glass.

"It's sweet," said the skinny sister.

Her mother winked.

Osiris sat back in his chair. He unbuttoned his pants, as he'd seen men do in movies. He reached his hand into his pants, as was suddenly his inclination. One of his mother's friends saw and looked away. She made a little sound like a rush of air. She drank some of her punch. Osiris burped and his mother turned and she said,

"Osiris!"

She immediately regretted this, though, as it caused everyone in the room to turn and discover Osiris, his hand buried deep beneath the waistline of his striped boxers, where he shuffled and tugged at himself, watching them drink their punch.

His mother grabbed him by the arm and pulled him out of the chair and into the other room.

"Not here," she said. Her eyes were a little slow in following the direction of her face. "Go to your room if you're done being in public. Don't embarrass me."

Osiris went into his room and his sister was there, eating her pizza.

"Michael is using my TV," she said.

Osiris said he wanted private time and his sister explained again that Michael was in her room, watching TV, and she needed a place to be.

Osiris walked over to her and plucked the pizza from her hand. He dropped it onto the carpet, pressed his foot into the cheese and toppings. He twisted his foot into the pizza and said, "Get out."

His sister started to cry.

"I'm hungry," she said.

"You're fat," said Osiris, and she kept crying.

The military men rang the doorbell. Osiris's mother answered the door and listened and took the paperwork and the flag and went back into the kitchen and told her friends her husband was dead.

"You're married?" said a friend. She scooped a citrus wedge with the punch spoon and dropped it into her cup.

Michael asked what happened. The skinny sister stared at the pizza. The fat sister wandered in and asked why everybody looked so different.

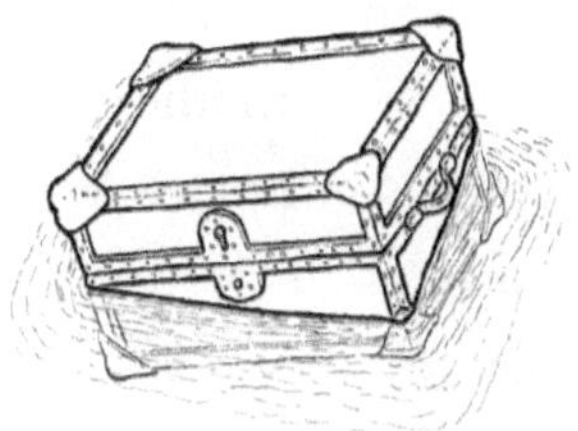

Their mother said they were broke. Osiris's skinny sister, Magdalene, got a job at Sonic. She wore roller skates, got tipped extra. She hated working there, thought she would get fat by just breathing the air. She considered working there for five hours the equivalent of two full meals. She walked to and from work. She walked the neighborhood. She flirted with the boys at Sonic. She gave a few of them hand jobs after work. But she didn't really like the boys at Sonic, so she stopped. When the summer came, college boys started showing up at Sonic. She worked later shifts, talked to the college boys. She liked older men because they had more to say than younger men. They made jokes, but didn't just make jokes. They said things like, "I'd really like to show you it," about the town where they grew up, or places they'd seen when they traveled. They said things like, "You'll see one day," and, "When you go there, make sure you..." These moments were the highlights of her shift.

She liked television. She watched several hours of television a day. She preferred stories in which the female lead exhibited confidence and charm. Her mother always talked about charisma, how Michael had charisma. Magdalene liked when the female lead acted like her brother Michael. They were all in high school together. Osiris did not do well socially or academically. He remained in special classes. Michael got by on his charm, for the most part. He played team sports. That meant a lot. He kept his grades up, somehow. They weren't great, but they were good enough. He ran track. He was voted *Nicest* his senior year. Magdalene had a certain following too. Claire, the other sister, was miserable in school and at home. She spent hours with Osiris, though he was almost always mean to her and moody.

Magdalene went home with one of the college boys. He gave her a drug in a white pill, and he took one too. The next morning, she was achy all over and thirsty and a little sad, but she got dressed and snuck out without waking him. His name was either Tim or Jim and he was a hunky linguistics major. She felt a little like a strong female lead, leaving as she did. She walked home and felt better by the time she was halfway there. She stopped at the Sonic on the way, checked her schedule. She had the day off, the next day too. It was rare they gave her weekends off, so she planned to make the best of it.

When she got home, her mother was waiting for her. Osiris and Claire were in the courtyard between the apartments, arguing. Michael had been out all night as well.

"Are you using protection?" asked their mother.

"Mom," said Magdalene.

"Sit down."

Magdalene sat. She crossed her legs, looked at her hands.

"Are you?"

Magdalene shook her head.

"Jesus, Maggie. Look. Do you know your options? Do you even know what you're doing? How much do you know?"

Magdalene shrugged. She pinched her belly.

"I need to take a shower," she said.

"Look, Honey," her mother placed her hands on her daughter's. "You just need to think it through is all."

Magdalene nodded.

"Do you know how to use a condom?"

She shrugged. "Don't they need to know that?"

"You need to know it too," said her mother. "Do you want to go on the pill? Do you know what that is?"

"I know what it does, Mom."

"It does more than you think it does."

"I know what it does," she said.

"Jesus Christ, Maggie. Oh Lord-God-Jesus-Christ and fucking piss."

That weekend Magdalene hid white wine in a water bottle and drank it in the grass by the public pool. She undid her top and lay on her belly. A young boy approached her and asked if she would turn over and she said, "Scram, you little pervert," even though part of her thought it might have been a fun thing to do.

Osiris and Claire had come to the pool with her, and they swam while she continued to sunbathe and drink more white wine. From a distance the boy yelled, "You're dumb as rocks."

She put her head down, closed her eyes.

Osiris peed in the pool and told Claire and she got out and spent the afternoon in the shade of the public pool's one tree, crying and prodding the ant piles with sticks she pulled loose from the branches. Osiris got out too and sat by Magdalene. He explained that he liked the water because it had shape and it didn't have shape and he could move all around inside of it, but it still held him up. He could close his eyes and sink himself and feel it all around him. He felt in and out of control.

Magdalene drank the entire bottle of white wine while Osiris talked to her.

"I peed in the pool," he said.

She took sip after sip.

After the wine was gone, Magdalene said they had to go. Osiris followed her willingly, but Claire refused to get up.

"Fine," said Magdalene. "Osiris..."

They left together. Claire stayed under the tree poking the ants, convinced they would come back. Magdalene left with no intention of coming back. She and her half-brother left the neighborhood in which the pool was located and wandered downtown. They stopped in a thrift store and went through the old records. Osiris found an old candy cane in a chest beneath a pile of sweaters and he put it in his pocket and broke off piece after piece, which he ate when he was convinced no one was looking. Magdalene found a dress she liked. It was white, with a floral pattern around the collar. She held it up against her in front of the mirror. Osiris said it looked nice. There was something in his mouth.

"What are you eating?"

Osiris shrugged. He went over to a box of toys and thumbed the G.I. Joes. Magdalene shoved the dress into her purse and grabbed Osiris by the elbow. She pulled him toward the door and he started to cry because he wanted to take the G.I. Joes with him but Magdalene explained that you do not always get the things you want in life, though she did not use those words exactly.

"Is he okay?" asked the clerk as she dragged him past the counter.

"He's fine," she said. "He's a little slow."

Outside, Osiris bit her on the wrist.

"I'm not slow," he said.

"You're dumb as rocks," Magdalene said. She rubbed her wrist, cursed him a few more times, and started to walk in the opposite direction. She wasn't headed anywhere in particular, just away from him.

Osiris picked up a rock by his foot and threw it at his older sister. She was already off balance, teetering from the adrenaline of the recent theft plus the bottle of wine on an empty stomach. When the rock struck, she collapsed. She hit the sidewalk like an egg. Her sweaty body made a soft smack, and she lay there, still, until Osiris finally approached. He was afraid, afraid of what she might do and of what he might have done. He wasn't a violent boy, wasn't typically angry about much, but he'd lost control. She rolled over and looked up at her brother. She started crying and told him she was pregnant, and he started crying because he didn't want to hurt the baby.

"You can't tell Mom," she said, and he swore he wouldn't.

That night she drank another bottle of white wine. She hated the taste of white wine but thought it would undo the pregnancy, so she drank it down like medicine. The police brought Claire home. She'd refused to leave the pool after closing and no one knew exactly where she came from or where she was going and she'd been too scared to tell them at first, but eventually one of the cops brought her a Red Rocket ice cream and she told them where she was from and where she was going and why she had refused to leave.

"You her sister?" the officer asked Magdalene. Their mother was asleep in the back room and the doorbell hadn't waked her. At least that's what Magdalene hoped.

"I'm her sister, yes. Our mother's asleep, but you can be sure we're all happy to see Claire alive and well and…"

"We'd prefer to talk with a legal guardian," explained the officer, "it would put our minds at ease to know her mother's assured of her safety."

"Well, she's sleeping," explained Magdalene.

Michael's car pulled up behind the police car, its lights still awhirl, and Michael climbed out and hurried to the front door.

"What happened?"

"You're the brother?"

"Claire refused to leave the pool and they called the cops on her," explained Magdalene. "Now they want to talk to Mom."

"Wake her up," said Michael. Michael talked to the police while Magdalene went to get their mother.

"Mom," Magdalene said. She put a hand on either of her mother's shoulders. "Mom. Get up."

Their mother didn't budge.

"Mom, the cops are here. Everything's fine. They just brought

Claire home because she wouldn't leave the pool."

Nothing.

"Mom." Magdalene shook their mother until her head began to bounce against the pillow. She looked around her for an empty bottle, liquor or pills. There was nothing. She shook her mother again.

"Stop it," said their mother.

Magdalene's hands came off.

"Your brother's taking care of it."

Magdalene realized then that the lights from the police car had shut off. The front door closed. Michael was talking to either Claire or Osiris. He made a joke. Claire erupted with hearty laughter.

"Do you have something you want to tell me?"

"No… Claire wouldn't leave, so we left…"

"You're pregnant. Osiris told me."

"So? So what?"

"That's why you've been stealing all the white wine? All the bourbon?"

She hadn't been stealing bourbon.

"It won't work," said her mother. "You're going to shit out a baby that's even dumber than you or whoever you let do this to you." Her mother sat up. "Sit down," she said.

Magdalene sat. She put her hands on her lap.

"Stop drinking. Start taking care of yourself. Do you know this boy at all?"

Magdalene shook her head.

"Okay. Does Michael know yet?"

She shook her head again.

"Okay."

When Magdalene had the baby, she had to quit Sonic. Michael got a job at a hardware store. He worked the morning hours. Their mother started selling their belongings online. Almost every appliance in the house was for sale. They had to be extra careful. If it wasn't screwed down or attached to a pipe or vent, she photographed it and put it online. Their sheets, their pillows, their toys, their microwave. All of it. The only exception was the television. They were tired all the time—they needed to relax. Plus, when the baby came, there was going to be a lot of stillness, a lot of time confined to a single room, and they would need something to get them through it. They sold the video games on the first day. The microwave, in a week. They sold all of Claire's stuffed animals and she was sad to see them go but was excited for the baby.

"For the baby," said their mother.

"For the baby," said Claire. She handed over her stuffed fox.

"For the baby," said their mother.

"For the baby," said Michael. He folded his leather jacket, placed it in the box.

"For the baby," said their mother.

"For William," said Magdalene. She took out her earrings. She borrowed her mother's old tops. She learned to make microwave popcorn on the stove. She cut her hair. She cancelled her plans for the tattoo at her ankle. She got her rest. She did not drink. She did everything her mother told her to do, everything she imagined her father might. She remembered her father. She saw him as a hero. A veteran. He'd fought so William could have the kind of life they'd always dreamed of having. Her father had died for that opportunity. She would die for it too. More than that, she would live.

William was born at seven pounds three ounces. As his mother remembered it, he was born fist raised to the air as if in mid-charge. It was a painful birth, she had forty-two stitches, but she hardly remembered them. She held William for nearly an hour after they cleaned him up without saying a word. He had blue eyes, a shroud of brown hair. He cried a little, but she could tell it was only because he hadn't learned the right words for the situation.

They brought the baby home and Claire loved the baby and Osiris loved the baby and their mother loved the baby and Michael was willing to help out here and there. When the baby was sleeping, everyone in the house was quiet. If Claire and Osiris got into it, it only took a gesture from their mother to send them outside where they could fight as loud as they wanted without disturbing the baby. The baby worked a kind of magic on the house. He charmed nearly everyone who entered. The baby's grandmother started laughing like she did when she was much younger. There was a smile on her face nearly all of the time. His grandmother laughed and laughed at nearly everything he did. His mother was weepy a lot of the time. She'd wanted him gone. She'd nearly lost him to herself. She couldn't get over it. But it didn't matter, because there he was.

Osiris wasn't allowed to babysit William. Neither was Claire. Michael was sometimes reluctant, but he agreed when he couldn't argue he needed rest for work. That was most often on the nights before his days off.

One Thursday, Michael made plans with Sheena, a girl he'd met in the parking lot of Chili's, where he and his friends gathered every now and then to talk out their plans for the evening. Magdalene and her mother were driving Claire to Fort Worth a two-week stay at a camp for underdeveloped girls. Claire would swim with other girls, learn to sew and make her own food. She would make friends. She would develop. Everyone in the family pitched in to provide this for her, and her sister and mother felt it was extremely important that they see her off. They'd driven her to several of these, though she never stayed away for more than a night.

Osiris was nearly eighteen. He was a quiet kid but wasn't trouble. Not really. Michael sat beside Osiris on the couch. They watched something in black and white with the volume turned low. William was sleeping. Michael had the phone in his palm in his lap. He had decided to call Sheena to cancel the date. Osiris laughed at the TV program. An overweight Black man in a cowboy outfit wandered from side to side in a saloon. A lean cowboy tried to trip him but slid on the puddle from a spilled beer. The overweight Black man began to laugh, and the other cowboys circled him. A brawl broke out and Osiris erupted into hearty laughter. Michael laughed a little too, to show his brother he was a good sport. He said, "Osiris, you're settled in for the night, right? You're not going out? You don't have plans?"

Osiris shook his head.

"Well, the thing is, I *do*. I have plans. I've got a date, and does it make sense to you that you're not supposed to watch the baby?"

Osiris shook his head again.

"Mom thinks I can't do it."

"See, and that's because she won't *let* you do it. She won't know you can handle it until you've *proven* you can handle it."

"How do I do that?"

"By watching William tonight. Just for an hour."

"You're watching William tonight."

"That's true. They asked me to."

They sat together a little longer, watched the show progress into a love scene. The main character sat outside a young woman's window, watched her brush her hair. She seemed to be singing, but the volume was too low to pick any of it out.

"He loves her," said Osiris.

"Have you ever been in love, Osiris?"

Osiris didn't take his eyes from the TV screen. He laughed a little. “Probably not,” said Michael. “I’m supposed to meet a girl tonight.”

The main character slid off his horse, crept closer to the window. He was right below the windowsill and the woman put her brush down, leaned out the window and over the hero. She appeared to sing, full volume into the evening, and the hero was riveted. His hands were shaking, his feet tapping. He reached up, grabbed her by the shoulders and pulled her down to him. She immediately began to hit him up and down, all over his body. Across the arms and the face and he took every blow until she wore out and paused to see who she was striking, who was allowing her to pummel him so. It was the stable boy, the man she thought she would never see again. She fell into his arms, and they held one another. The scene faded to black.

“What does she look like?” asked Osiris.

“Who?”

“The girl.”

“Who? Sheena? She looks like… she looks Italian, I guess.”

“Like her?” Osiris pointed to the heroine, who was now in a dimly lit apple orchard, plucking apples from a tree barely within her reach.

“Sure,” said Michael. “I guess. Sort of like her.”

They watched the movie a little longer, then Michael got up.

“You’re going to be alright?” he asked.

“I’m alright,” said Osiris.

“You’re going to mind after William? Feed him if he’s hungry? Walk him around if he’s crying?”

Osiris nodded, watched the TV. Michael left.

After the movie was over, Osiris headed into William’s room. The baby was sleeping on his back, head to the side. He moved his hand a little. Drool came out. Osiris leaned against the bars of the cage. They bent beneath his weight. His breath came hot and heavy over the baby while it slept. The baby had fat little legs. Its legs looked too fat for its pants. The fat bubbled out over the hem of his shorts. Osiris reached in, pinched the baby on the inside of its thigh. Nothing happened. He pinched a little harder and the baby squirmed. William brought his arm down, his leg up. His face puckered and he began to cry. Osiris pinched again, and the baby screamed. Osiris reached in and lifted his nephew into his arms. The baby cried and cried in his arms and Osiris bounced him and spun his way down the hall whispering, *shhh*, until finally the baby got quiet again. Osiris placed the baby back in its bed and watched it move around. He lifted a small stuffed ball to his mouth, pressed it against his gums. Osiris sneezed onto the baby and he started crying again, bawling, and Osiris lifted him again, but this made the baby cry harder. Osiris bounced the baby and spun the baby and sang songs into the baby's ears, but it did no good. Osiris played the record his mother had left in the player and when the music kicked up, William finally settled down. He pressed into Osiris' shoulder as he spun and bounced the baby, singing along.

Two hours later, Magdalene and her mother arrived. Michael was nowhere to be seen. Osiris had William in his lap on the couch. A war show was on, and the men were talking about how your unit becomes your friends and your friends become your family. You're in a war with your whole family and one day the bullets rain down and two-thirds of your family is ripped apart and you're surrounded by dead men you love but never really knew and Osiris was crying a little but held it back when his mother walked in.

"Where's Michael?" she asked.

"He's gone for an hour," said Osiris. "He'll be right back."

"That son of a bitch," said Magdalene. She scooped up William and asked him over and over again if he was alright. The baby burbled and she said, "You're alright. You're alright."

The next morning Osiris climbed on top of the house. Everyone except for Magdalene was asleep, but they were one after the other roused from sleep by the heavy clomping of Osiris's booted feet. Magdalene went out first, William in arm, to investigate the sound, and there was Osiris, on the roof, his arms spread wide like a goose in flight.

"Bring me the baby," he said.

"You're out of your mind," Magdalene said. She went inside.

"Who's on the roof?" asked their mother.

"Osiris is out of his mind," said Magdalene.

“Sy’s on the roof?” said Michael.

“Come on down, buddy.” Michael held one hand at his eyes to shield them from the sun, the other was at his hip. He was shirtless, in shorts. “Come down from there.”

“I’m going to jump because no one trusts me,” said Osiris.

“You’re not going to jump, Sy.”

“I am going to jump.”

“You’re not going to jump because if you jump, and you survive, I’ll break your legs.”

“Get down,” said their mother. She tightened her robe and stepped down from the porch. “Listen to your brother. You’re upsetting the baby.”

“What about Maggie?”

“You’re upsetting Maggie too, now get down.”

“Bring me William.”

“We’re not bringing the baby on the roof, Sy. Get the hell down from there.”

“I’m not getting down,” said Osiris. “I’m jumping down.”

“Sy, it’s a fifteen-foot jump. If you jump, you’ll just sprain an ankle. Get the hell down from there.”

Osiris leapt. He landed on his face, his chest, his knees, toes, and wrists. He broke a wrist and bruised his face.

“No one trusts me,” he told the doctor.

The doctor stretched his mouth against his teeth and shone a light in Osiris’s eyes.

“Stop jumping from rooftops. Might be a step in the right direction.” The doctor touched his knee and rose up. He smiled, said goodbye, and let Osiris’s mother in. She drove him home in silence.

At the house, she stopped him in the hall. She hit him once across the mouth and asked him if he knew how much this was going to cost them. He shook his head.

"You didn't think about it, did you? We're paying for this bullshit. Your little bullshit, we're paying for it."

He shook his head.

"You think we're not paying for it? You think it's free?" She raised her hand to hit him again but stopped herself. She brought her hand down.

He shook his head. He was crying a little. She slapped the broken wrist.

"You shit." She left him there leaning against the wall and went to pick up Claire, who was struggling at the camp and needed to come home, as usual.

The next morning everyone was gathered around the kitchen table.

"We're not sending him to a home," Michael said.

"We're not keeping him here," said Magdalene. "Not with William around. Not with you leaving them alone together we're not."

"Are you blaming me?"

"Someone put all this in his head."

"If you put even the slightest bit of faith in him..."

"Then what? Then what, Michael? He would have flown?"

Claire laughed at that, though Magdalene was yelling and the baby was crying.

They visited Osiris once a month as a group. They convinced him the facility was in his best interests. No one wanted to see him go, they said, but they wanted him to get better. They wanted him to be able to spend more time with William. They wanted William to grow up around an older brother who was safe and secure and happy. They didn't want William to grow up around a brother who was jumping off rooftops. The facility was more than they could afford, and Michael took on a second job as night manager at a Dairy Queen. Magdalene got Claire a job at the Sonic. She still knew a few people. Claire refused to wear the skates. She got few tips. She made few friends. Customers complained about her attitude, her clothing stains, how often and how badly she screwed up the orders. Claire ate on the job. She spilled food on the floor purposefully so she could eat what they would otherwise throw away. She took smoke breaks, though she didn't smoke. During those breaks, she sat on her hand at the picnic table behind the building. She dug her hand past the loose belt around her waist, the elastic of her underwear. She farted on her hand and sat there for the full ten minutes. She did not offer service with a smile.

"You're going to get fired," Osiris said. They were gathered together around a circular table. He was all in white. "If they catch on to how little you care, they're going to fire you."

"Maybe," Claire said.

Their mother was at the vending machine, trying to buy five ice creams. The machine took her dollar in, whirred, and spat it out. She tried again.

"You need to give a shit," Magdalene said. She took out her breast, drew William to it.

"You're doing that here?" Michael said.

"Everyone's getting ice cream. Why can't he eat?"

"That baby is nearly a year old, Maggie."

"He likes it."

"It's disgusting."

"Shut the fuck up, Michael, and go have your own kid."

"Goddamn this piece of shit. Does anyone have a dollar?" Their mother was sweating, her sunglasses atop her head. "Do any of you have a dollar?" None of them did. Their mother was in possession of nearly every penny they earned. "Well, then I'll go without, I guess." She passed an ice cream to Michael, Osiris, Claire, and Magdalene.

"We'll split, Mom." Osiris broke the sandwich in half.

"You're my sweet boy," she said. She licked the sides first, brought the edges of the cookie together. "Mama's sweet boy."

"I wish Dad could be here." Osiris looked to the grated window, where there was nothing to see. Michael watched his brother turn.

“What are you looking at?”

Their mother said nothing.

“If Dad was here,” Osiris said, “this would be our TV moment.”

William coughed. A dribble of milk fell to the curve of Magdalene’s shirt, unbuttoned and hanging.

“I love you five very much,” said their mother.

“We love you, Mom,” said Michael.

“Yeah,” said Osiris.

Claire nodded, finished her ice cream sandwich.

Magdalene said she loved her more than anything in the whole entire world.

They felt the room expand around them, as if someone were watching them, and had just taken a step back. The rest of the people in the room felt very far away, distant and indistinct.

“Here’s to Raul,” said their mother. She closed her mouth

around the final bite of the ice cream sandwich.

"Here's to William," she said, and wiped her mouth.

William grew and grew. In grade school, he was the tallest kid in his class by several inches. He had thick arms, even as a boy. By middle school, he was a quarterback. Michael taught him to toss a spiral in the backyard. Osiris was out of the facility. He was quieter than ever, but peaceful. Claire had been fired from Sonic and found a job at a snow cone stand just down the road. She drank cups of the syrup when no one was looking. She brought them back to William and he took packets of the stuff on long runs. He was running in the mornings, working out in the evening. The boy was a machine. They'd never seen anything like it.

"His father was pretty hunky if I recall," Magdalene said to her mother one afternoon. They were watching the boy climb a tree in the backyard. He climbed until the branches grew thin, dropped down and climbed again. Magdalene's mother laughed and batted her hand.

William never knew his father. His mother had grown up

without a father too, and he had two uncles who wouldn't leave him alone, so he didn't think about it much. He wrestled with Osiris, played games with Michael. Michael was managing the hardware store where he worked and was taking night classes. He was exhausted most of the time but loved watching William get worked up. Magdalene and her mother took up smoking together. They drank in the afternoons and watched their boys play and wrestle and they felt genuinely happy and content. They plumped up together. Claire bloated. Osiris chubbed up as well. Michael stayed lean and muscular, and William was bursting at the seams. His veins were piano wire.

William and Michael drank beers on the back porch after dark. Osiris sat with them sometimes, but he never touched the stuff.

"You really jumped off the roof?" asked William.

Michael lifted his eyebrow, looked to Osiris.

"I did," said Osiris. "I wouldn't recommend it."

Michael laughed and Osiris laughed a little too. William watched them both. He wanted to understand his uncles, but there was something off about them. He never felt quite at home with them, but he enjoyed himself, nonetheless. There was something missing, but he didn't know what. He'd never known anything but this, so he had nothing to measure it against. He asked for another beer and Osiris served him from the cooler underneath him.

"What was your dad like?" William asked.

"He was great," Osiris said.

"We didn't know him that well," said Michael.

"Dad was a hero," Osiris said.

"That's true," said Michael. "He was that."

The next morning, the television was gone. The front door was open. Mud streaked the carpet. Michael called the police, and they came and filed a report.

"Let us know if you find anything out," they said.

The day after that, the rainy-day money was gone. Their

mother kept a curl of bills in a coffee can in her sock drawer. She'd gone in to file away a quarter of Claire's paycheck from the snow cone stand, but the can was missing. She'd burst into Osiris's room and demanded he return the money, but he insisted he had nothing, knew nothing of what she was talking about. Michael asked him once, in private, if he'd seen the money, maybe noticed it out of place somewhere, which made Osiris cry and insist further he didn't know what they were talking about.

"Maggie?" asked their mother.

"Fuck you," Magdalene said. She left the room.

William came home from school to find everyone in a rough mood. Osiris had locked himself in the room he shared with William. Michael was in the backyard, smoking and drinking beer and working on the lawn mower. Magdalene was splitting a piecrust with Claire, who was sweating in a tank top opposite her sister. Their mother was on the phone with the police.

"That's twice this week," she said. "It's an epidemic. What are you going to do about it? What am *I* supposed to do about it? We can't live like this! Don't you think I've thought of…"

She saw William, smiled at the boy, and left the kitchen for the laundry room, closed the cord in the door.

“What’s going on?”

“We got robbed,” said Claire.

“I know.”

“Again.”

William didn’t tell anyone, but he stayed up the entire night the night after the second theft. He waited until everyone fell asleep. He closed his eyes while Osiris rocked himself to sleep in the bed across from him, and he left the room. He set himself up in a chair in the living room, across from the door. The hours passed. He watched. He imagined all the great things he could do. The door opened and a masked stranger walked in. He grabbed the guy by his throat, body slammed him. Crushed his neck with his foot. The door opened, a masked stranger leapt in. There was no one in the room. William dropped onto him from above. He broke his neck in three places. He dragged the corpse out onto the lawn and pierced it through with a stake. He stabbed the stake into the ground and stood back. A masked bad guy entered the house through a window. William broke the window and shut it before the guy got his leg through, and William chopped the leg clean off. He dragged the one-legged crook into the living room and kicked him to death in front of Magdalene, Claire, his grandmother, and Michael. Osiris guarded the back door. A masked bad guy entered the house to find no one in it. There was nothing to steal either. The house was an empty shell. He turned to leave, but William slammed the door, bolted it. He lit the oily rags and the house erupted into flame around the bad guy. The bad guy pressed his face to the glass windows in the living room, but he hadn't the strength to break the glass. He begged for his life, but William was unmoved. The bad guy collapsed into the flame and was consumed. They collected the insurance money and William built them a nicer, two-story house atop the ashes of their old house and the bad guy who'd tried to mess with them. He imagined all the great things he could do, and the sun rose behind him, and his mother woke to find him asleep on a wooden chair across from the door.

She nudged him awake.

"Do you want breakfast?"

He nodded.

"Do you think violence is good?" he asked.

Magdalene broke an egg into a bowl.

"What do you mean?"

"I mean to protect yourself. Or people you love?"

"Do I think it's *good?*" She broke a second egg.

"Yeah."

"Yes. To protect yourself and your family. Yes, I do."

"And people you love."

"Do you love someone?"

"Sure."

"Someone outside the family." A third egg.

"No."

“Eighth graders don’t date seventh graders, Mom.”

“My apologies,” she said.

“Unless you just want to score.”

Magdalene laughed, poked the edge of the omelet, and then looked very sad.

“Are you scoring?” she asked.

William shrugged.

“Are you trying to score?”

“Mom.”

“I should know these things. You can tell me.”

“I just said I wasn’t just trying to score.”

“You didn’t say that,” she said. She flipped the eggs.

“More or less, I did.”

“Who do you love?” She whisked the three eggs in a bowl with milk.

“No one.”

“Who do you *like*, then?”

“You make it sound like there should only be one.” William sat up in his seat, looked away from his mother pouring eggs and milk into the pan.

“Oh ho, I see. Well, give me the list. Is Sheila on there?”

“Sheila?”

“The girl I saw you with the other day. The girl who walked you home.”

“She’s in seventh grade, Mom.”

“Okay.”

“That’s a year below me.”

“I’m well aware.”

“Okay. You know I love you, right?” she said.

“Mom, yes.”

“And you know I couldn’t be happier with you, right?”

“Yes, Mom.”

“Well, it was a very significant struggle having you, William. Our family wasn’t ready. I wasn’t ready. It was very hard.”

“Okay.”

“I’m just saying make sure you’re ready is all.” She slid the eggs onto a plate, cut them in half and gave them to William with a fork. “Orange juice?”

“How do I know I’m ready?”

“When you start to feel it, wait two years. If you still feel it, you’re ready.”

He ate the eggs. She watched. Two weeks later, there was another break-in. They put tape over Claire’s mouth and held her down. They poured gasoline on her. They weren’t there to rob anyone. They lit a match. They'd been caught the month before. They'd robbed a liquor store in Sanger and accidentally killed the clerk. They were out on bail, awaiting trial. They dropped the match. She had no money. They trashed her room. They tore up books, shredded clothes, the sheets. One punted her goldfish in its bowl. It hit the wall with a thud, fell to the ground and spilled. The house burned around them. They kicked open the window and climbed out to escape the smoke. The goldfish flipped, flipped again.

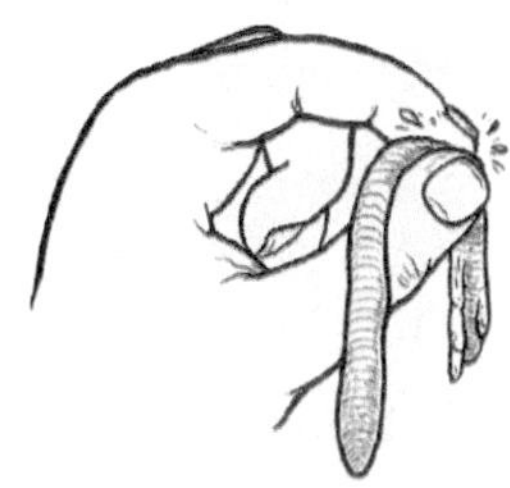

William's theory with gun shows was that you should always bring a gun.

"There's no telling what kind of maniacs are walking around those places armed," he'd say.

He preferred pistols. He liked knives. Close-range weapons.

He worked at the local high school, as an art teacher. He enjoyed metalworking, bas-relief. He wrote spiritual poetry, which he called *sermons*. His girlfriend was a marathon runner.

He was at a gun show when the hospital called to tell him his girlfriend had water poisoning. So, he wound up bringing a pistol downtown, to the hospital nearest where she had finished the race. She hadn't stayed hydrated during the race and when she finished, she drank and she drank and she drank and she collapsed. William brought his pistol into the back room of the emergency room and leaned in to kiss his girlfriend, who was sleeping.

"Love you, sweetheart," he said, and he left to go find balloons or flowers or something before she came to.

When he came back, a stuffed dragon under one arm, she'd switched rooms. He wandered the halls looking for her and before he found her, he happened across a room around which a large number of people were gathered. A line had even formed at the door, and people of all ages were going in and out, their heads hung low.

"Who's in there?" he asked a passing nurse. She shrugged. William got in line, if only to stand on his toes and see into the room. There was an elderly man in a bed there, and people gathered around him. He was talking to each of them, one after the other. He held their hands, kissed their palms. A few of the women were crying, a few of the men. William was moving forward in the line. Were these friends? Family? Was this a celebrity? If he got inside and the man spoke to him, what would he say? William inched forward until finally he entered the room. He took a spot by the old man in the bed. He needed to be by his girlfriend's side, not this stranger's, but it had all happened very fast.

"Father," said the man beside him, "I feel lost. I feel that life is too much for me. My kids are growing up. My wife is… she's not the woman I married." The man's head hung low.

"You must learn to appreciate what you have," said the old man. He took the other man's hand in his. "This moment. The unpredictable next. These are worth more than any dream you might have, any fantasy about what you could be doing or should be doing. A life-force moves through you, pulls you along, and you are me before you know it. And you will die."

It was William's turn next. The old man turned to him. His face curled up a bit.

"You're a new face." He shifted in his bed, placed his hands on either side of his frail body and pushed it higher up against the pillow behind him. "Are you a cousin?"

William nodded.

"I'm glad you came," said the old man. He took William's hand in his, held it. He closed his eyes.

William sensed he was about to move on, to greet the woman beside him. William did not want him to break contact. There was something extremely comforting in the man's kindness, his small body, his weak state. The man was so far from threatening. He was a spider web, the loose thread at the hem of a shirt. The man was next to nothing with his hands on William's.

"I, um, I brought you this," said William. He withdrew his hands and brought the stuffed dragon out from under his arm.

"Why thank you." The old man held the dragon out before him. "A dragon," he said.

William left. He found his girlfriend's room, in another hall. She was asleep when he entered. She was to be released in the morning. They wouldn't allow him to stay the night.

William went back to the gun show. There were a few more hours left, but people were packing their booths up early. He caught two men as they folded the long table that had held their literature on a new scope for William's preferred pistol. He talked them into giving him a few discount codes for their website.

He sat in the backyard with a BB gun for the rest of the afternoon, shot cans lined up along the fence. He loaded the gun, pumped until it was painful to push, and fired. The cans went flying. He drank beers and loaded the gun. A stray dog was sniffing one of the dropped cans. William pumped the gun. A car passed in front of the house and the dog moved away from the can, toward the field that opened up out of William's backyard. It was state land, marked off with a barbed wire fence, but it was an old fence. The dog slid through, and William watched it go. He went to the garage and found a shovel. He dug for an hour or so, a ditch in the backyard. He climbed inside. About knee deep and a few feet wide. He dug a little more because it felt good on his arms. The next morning, he had to work. The ditch was a little deeper now. He climbed inside. He knelt and examined the mud walls. The end of an earthworm dangled there, and he plucked it with his fingers, broke it loose from its front and brought it to his eye. The earthworm worked all the time. Or it never worked. He pressed his fingers together, smeared the earthworm between them.

His girlfriend's mother picked her up in the morning. William went to work.

When he got home, he had several messages on his answering

machine. One was from his uncle Osiris. His cat was sick, needed medication and fluids daily. The doctor had once given the cat three weeks, but Osiris kept it alive for another two years. The phone call was an update on the cat's behavior. She was moodier than usual. She wasn't eating much. He was worried. The next message was from William's mother. He skipped it. The next was an automated voice. He let it play out while he scrubbed the cups and the bowls in the sink. He pried the dried food loose with his fingernails. The voicemail ended. His girlfriend clicked on. She was feeling better. The whole thing was terrifying. She'd thought she was going to die. She could have died. You don't get many second chances in life. She kept on like that for a few minutes, until she said she was ready to move on. She and William had been growing apart for some time now. She was pregnant. She didn't want any help. She hung up.

William had a drink. He called Osiris and let him talk about the cat for nearly an hour. William drank. What was left of the day dimmed. Osiris asked him to come visit and William said that, yeah, he might do that.

James made William call him Rad. He lived in a trailer at the top of a hill beside one of the busier country roads. He had built a little porch for himself, out of the back of the trailer, facing the hills. There was cattle land in one direction, country roads and a highway in the other.

"Babies are like these little worms that crawl out of them and started wriggling around and growing and they shit out a few other worms of their own along the way before they crawl into the ground and fall apart there." Rad loaded the skeet shooter and looked to William.

"Pull," said William.

He pulled the trigger and the disc shattered. Flakes of clay fell, and William released his body into the lawn chair.

"See," Rad said. "I told you you'd feel better."

"I'd like to do something for them still," said William.

"She doesn't want any help, Will." Rad loaded the launcher. He took the gun out of William's hand and broke the neck. He popped the empty shells and loaded two more from his pocket. He placed the empty shells in the twelve-pack at his feet, half-empty itself. William crouched by the launcher.

"I know," he said.

He released the disc and Rad watched it fly. He turned slightly, matched the movement, got a lead, then fired. The disc disintegrated.

"Well," Rad said. "What did you have in mind?"

"I don't know," William said. "Money."

"Because what else would she want?"

William thought about the stuffed dragon. Maybe if he had brought her the stuffed dragon instead of giving it to that dying man who was probably dead right now. Maybe then he could have been there when the baby was born. Maybe then he could have…

"Your turn." Rad loaded the launcher. He handed the shotgun to William who propped it against his shoulder. He leaned forward in his chair.

"Are you still friends with that guy at the QT?"

"Randy, yeah."

"What kind of money on hand?"

"A thousand until eight. You're interested now?" Rad set the shotgun down on its butt.

"No," said William. He took the gun.

Rad loosed the disc and William fired. The disc soared on, arced toward the ground, and faded into the grass.

There were two men in the QT, other than Randy, when William pulled the pistol. He told them to get down, told Randy to keep his hands up. William climbed over the counter and had Randy open the register. One of the men rose up and fired on the two of them. Randy fell. William fired back, landed two in the man's chest. The other man covered his head and stared into the linoleum. William climbed over the counter and checked the man's pulse. Randy pressed a silent alarm. William found a spot of blood on his shirt, so he removed it, tore open the clear packaging that held a T-shirt boasting the colors and emblem of a local sports team. He put on the new shirt, grabbed a handful of cash from the drawer, and exited. He hadn't thought it through. Things hadn't gone right. He walked to the corner, where there was a bus stop. He waited only a few minutes, climbed onto the bus when it arrived. It held to the curb a moment, waiting for the police cars to pass before it could continue.

William rode the bus for about an hour. He got out under an overpass and walked around to the stairs leading to the walking path that led out of town, into the next. He walked a few miles, an hour or so, and stopped when he saw a motel. He crossed the highway, crossed the access road, entered the motel sweating and panting and asked the man behind the thick glass if they took cash.

William collapsed into his stiff bed. The springs coiled into him. He emptied his pockets, counted the money. A couple hundred. A week or so.

In the morning, he left the motel. He walked a few miles in the heat, stopped at a restaurant. He ordered three tacos and a plate of rice and beans. He scooped the rice and beans into his mouth with the tacos, wiped his fingers across the plate, and left. Once outside, he jogged a little down the street, ducked behind another restaurant. He followed the path there through to the other side of the street, poked his head out, looked both ways, and continued on into the trees. Beyond the main drag of this town, there was the country. A few houses dotted the landscape, but he kept his distance from them, moved through the fields, stopped every now and then at a tree for shade.

For the first time in his life, William was totally alone. It was exciting, if not terrifying. He would need some money. That was the first order of business. And then some clothes. Eventually, food. He kept on through the fields until he hit a road. He chose left and headed that way. Cars passed, but he didn't hitch. There was no way of telling who was driving and he didn't want to take any unnecessary chances. It wasn't exactly safe, following a main road, but he needed to get into town somewhere, somehow. He needed to put together some money, maybe find a place to crash for the night. The first thing he came across was a gas station, but he walked right past it. Next, a grocery store. It was early afternoon at that point. A woman was wheeling her groceries out to the car in a cart, and he offered to help.

"No, thank you, I'll be just fine," she said. She kept on, a little faster now.

He leaned against one of the bigger cars in the lot, shielded himself from the sun and from the view of the entrance. How did people make quick money in this town? He eyed a couple counting change in their car.

"You two looking to make a buck?" he asked.

They weren't.

William started checking doors. He tested five locked cars before one gave. He climbed into a champagne minivan, checked the dash and between the front seats for stored cash. Nothing. He checked the driver's side panel and found a pack of cigarettes. He didn't smoke, tossed them. He climbed into the backseat and waited. An elderly man opened the trunk of the van and loaded his groceries. William was curled in the backseat, still as he could be. The old man climbed into the front seat and started the car. He reached for his cigarettes and William sat up. William told the man he had a gun, to be still, to empty his pockets. The old man shifted in his seat. He pulled his wallet out, dropped it. His arms were shaking. He was making soft sounds with his mouth. William told him to get the wallet. He leaned over, sat back up and shot William in the face.

The old man called the police from a stranger's cell phone.

He'd almost forgotten the gun was there. The gun had seemed to pull itself out. He'd only turned. Then the criminal's face had peeled back. His ears were ringing. He couldn't hear the operator's questions. The police came and took his information. They matched William's gun to the gun that shot the clerk back at the QT. They phoned William's mother. She sent his uncle.

Osiris showed up at the morgue nearly an hour and a half late. His feet were taped. He had on a knee brace.

"When I walk," he explained, "my knee turns slightly to the right. I can feel it with every step. Anyway, it's been getting sore. So, I wear the brace. The brace clicks. It disturbs the cat. So, I tape it. I tape the other one, or else my walk is off."

The guy at the morgue asked Osiris if he was ready to identify the body.

There was little to identify. His face was cleared from the eyes down. His mouth, gone. A tooth or two clung here and there, as if weeded through. The body had William's eyes, though. William's hair.

"That's him," said Osiris. "He was supposed to come over

yesterday and he never came over. My cat gets nervous when I'm having visitors. I try to clean up a little bit and that makes her nervous. So, I didn't clean for him. I was feeling guilty today about it, because my cat seemed nervous anyway. Maybe she can just tell when someone's coming over. Or when I think someone is coming over. Because he never came. My mom says I should put her down. But there's enough cruelty in the world without us going out of our way to kill our pets."

William's daughter was born Mary Louise. Her grandmother and great aunt and uncles were not alerted to her birth. William's girlfriend, the marathon runner, moved in with her great uncle Joseph and they went about raising Mary Louise. Joseph was an ex-army man. He received a pension. He was retired after forty-five years of work at Texas Instruments. Now he bought cars, fixed them up, and sold them. He walked everywhere he needed to go.

Mary Louise was a striking blonde from the day she was born. She had brilliant blue eyes like her daddy. Her mother talked to her about her daddy from time to time. She did not want to keep any secrets from the girl. She told her that her daddy had gone the wrong way, but she was bound to go the right way.

Her daddy had been a good man, though. But good men didn't always stay good, that was one of the most important things she could ever learn. There were no guarantees. Everything changed in unpredictable ways, even the best things. Mary Louise needed to love what she had and be ready to let it go. Her mother loved her very much. That was the one exception to the rule. As long as she was living, Mary Louise would be her number one thing.

She sang to the baby, talked to the baby. The baby slept in her arms. Her great uncle Joseph, now Gran Joe, paced the kitchen. He put away dishes, swept the floor. He asked if they needed anything. They didn't. They rarely did. Or when they did, they were sure to ask him. He rarely caught them in a quiet moment of need.

Mary Louise grew up alongside her mother and her Gran Joe. She learned to ask questions and she stopped her Gran Joe in his tracks one day when she looked up at him, past the arc of the hose he'd pointed in her direction, and said,

"Gran Joe, you're making me angry."

"She's an angel," said Gran Joe.

The men in Gran Joe's family had been military for as long as he had records. Generation after generation enlisted, were drafted, served. Never above a foot soldier, not one of them. Some of them died. Some lived and died later. He had letters from a few to their wives, mistresses, lovers. He sometimes read them to Mary Louise as bedtime stories.

Sweetheart, I'm thinking of you always. I hate to march. I complain about it every day. I complain often. The other men don't understand. You have always been sweet to me. You're my good listener. I miss how you listen. Love.

"Your great-great-grandfather was killed in combat by friendly fire," Gran Joe said.

"Is there a war going on right now, Gran Joe?"

"Not really," he said. "Not here. Not one you have to worry about." He kissed her on the head.

"One more?" she asked.

Darling, I wake each morning to thoughts of you. But they are bothered, pushed aside by the idea of my wife, your husband. Imagine if, when I return, we were rid of them. Imagine walking down the streets together, hand-in-hand, and proud of it. Imagine the things we would say to one another in public. Imagine if you spilled your drink in front of the waiter, and we laughed, and you were embarrassed and I could tell you I love you. Imagine how often I could tell you I love you. I would drown you in them. It is starting to rain. Each drop is a kiss from you. I am telling myself that. The ink is running, and I must go. I will make no great attempt to escape from the rain today, because I love you. I love you.

"This one was from a distant cousin of yours. He went to war to avoid cancer, survived the war, then died of cancer."

"How many people that you know have died?"

"Well, Mary Louise… most of them."

"We all have to die?"

"Yes."

"I have to die?"

"Yes."

"Not now?"

“Not now, and not tomorrow and not any time soon.”

“Will you be there when I die?”

“I hope not.”

“Will you read one more?”

“Gladly, Miss Louise.”

Son, you're going to read this upon my death. Maybe months after, maybe only a few days. Maybe the war will be over, maybe it will never end. It feels end-less. I feel sometimes like we're walking in circles. I'm writing because I think about you all the time. Not because I have anything in particular to say. Or maybe I have a few things to say, but it's not the kind of thing I thought I'd be putting in a letter. When you grow up, you're going to be handsome. You might not notice it at first. Girls will like you more than your friends and you might not notice that either.

Treat your friends well. They'll be around for longer. At least at first. Treat women well, too, I'm not saying you shouldn't. Treat them very well, but when you're young, you'll date more than a few, I'm sure and most of them won't be worth the time it takes you to realize that. You'll have kids of your own one day. And they'll grow up fast. Life moves very fast. It's unbearable. Sometimes I look back over the things I've done, the things I've seen, even in the past year, and it seems one great big joke. Like nothing lasts even a moment. Just one thing then the next and it's all so fine and terrifying too.

War is a waste of time, son. If you can avoid it, do so. If you have to cut off your pinkie, do it. I would cut off my pinkie this instant if it meant I got to be back home with you and your mom tomorrow. In life, the best you can hope for is that you find something you love to watch change. I love watching you change. You and your mother. She used to have a different hair color, even. Her hair was blonde when I met her, not that I don't like the brown. But she was a blonde bombshell, that's the scientific term. She was the confidence I'd always lacked. She scooped me up and cut my hair and I was in love with her then and I'm even more in love now. I think about you two all the time. Every minute. It's an adventure out here, that's for sure. But I do not like it. It's an adventure back home, you'll see that soon enough.

Watch your friends, the paths they take. Watch the people around you and the way their lives change. Never fool yourself into thinking it's the same thing day after day, or else you'll wake up one morning and look back over your life and be struck suddenly with all the things you missed. You'll be in a strange place; you'll be a strange person. You'll have no sense of how you got where you are, what you're doing or why. Because you stopped paying attention. I stopped paying attention. Look at me now.

There are magnolia trees here. Would you believe it? Just like at home. Magnolias in bloom. Their leaves turn pink and drop into a circle around the base of their trunk. The men I'm with kick through the circles as we pass. The leaves are like banana peels. You can press them with your boot, draw out a little bit of the liquid still in their veins. It leaves an oily streak wherever you trace your foot. These are some of the small pleasures afforded us on a daily basis. Look for those, okay? When you can't find them, change something. Something drastic. Something you think you can't. I love you, son. I'll see you soon.

"He shot himself in the leg."

Mary Louise was asleep, but she woke up, sat up.

"Put a bullet in his leg and was dishonorably discharged because everyone knew that he did it, and why he did it."

Mary Louise rubbed her eyes.

"He was your great granduncle. My grandfather's brother."

"I want to meet them."

"Me too, sweetheart."

❦

"I dreamed last night that I met the men in Gran Joe's letters," said Mary Louise.

Her mother poured apple juice into a plastic cup with a screw top lid.

"I went to where you go when you die and met all of Gran Joe's family."

"What did they say," asked her mother. She sat at the table where Mary Louise was finishing her pancakes.

"That I didn't have to die and be like them if I didn't want to." She picked up the last wedge of pancake and spun it on the end of her fork, twirling the syrup.

Gran Joe was in the other room, puttering around the television, the bookcase, the pile of toys.

"You certainly don't have to worry about it now," said her mother. Her mother folded the edge of the tablecloth in front of her.

Mary Louise dropped the wedge of pancake into the layer of syrup. Her mother stood, bent, touched her toes, and hung there for a minute.

"Did you stretch this morning?" she asked.

"I stretched," said Mary Louise.

"Did you finish your breakfast?" She rose up, vertebrae by vertebrae.

Mary Louise held out the last bite. "Want it?"

Her mother shook her head, sat on the floor and reached out to her feet.

Mary Louise grew up at an astonishing rate. She was tall, muscular like her father. She liked soccer but didn't pursue organized sports after middle school. She went on runs with her mother but tended to stop early. She dieted with her mother but tended to cheat. Her mother had a schedule on the wall, an enormous calendar. Which foods when, how far to run, which parts of the body needed attention on which days. Gran Joe was always saying what beautiful, dedicated angels had flown into his life. He was healthy for an old-timer. He didn't smoke, didn't drink. Worked in the yard most of time. Mary Louise came home from a run and found him moving sticks around in the backyard. He followed her in, poured a glass of water, offered a bite of food. He was waiting for her, for her mother. He didn't do much else.

On weekdays, Mary Louise studied most of the night. At school, she told her friends she had a photographic memory. She debated. She took the advanced classes, did well in them. She decided she was going to be a poet. She sat under mesquite trees. She watched ticks climb the tall grass, hang from the tip of each blade. She noticed dogs taking naps, and how they sometimes yipped. Everything that came out of her was dark and painful to read. She wrote about blood and burning barns. She imagined miscarriages, leaned heavily on the imagery of the ticks. Women were birthing dead babies in the next town over. There was something in the water. She showed only one friend these early poems. He told her they were all great, each one better than the previous.

"You think so?" she said. It was morning. They met on the back porch, walked to school together. She plucked a dead mosquito from her coffee. "Like book-good?"

"Like anthology-good," he said. He was always encouraging

her to go swimming. "What are you doing today?"

She shrugged. He was ditching, going to the lake.

At the lake Mary Louise spread out a towel like a blanket. She'd brought a bag full of books and drew them out to her side. She read a little here and there, watched her friend swim, dive forward into the water. He encouraged her to get in, but she shook her head.

"At least get some sun," he said.

She was in jean shorts and a T-shirt. She removed the T-shirt, and he gave her a thumbs-up. She wrote two poems in the margins of two books. She made a point of writing a poem whenever she had the opportunity. She firmly believed she was getting better with each poem. Maybe each poem wasn't better than the last, as her friend insisted, but she was learning new things, trying things out. Her hand moved more easily. She thought a little less. She was excited for the gap to close between thinking and writing. She was excited for the first poem she wouldn't have to make herself write, or at least think to write, think her way through. She was excited to channel something. She was excited for the muscle memory. Her friend lay beside her, on the side opposite the books.

"Sunscreen?" he asked.

She turned over, allowed him to press sunscreen into and around the strap of her bathing suit top. He paid special attention to the shoulders, to her sides, curled his fingers around to her abdomen.

"That tickles," she said.

He returned his hands to her back. With a subtle pinch, he unclipped the top of her suit. The strap split, fell to either side of her. She started to sit up and he ran his thumbs along either side of her spine.

"It's easier this way," he said. "Just stay down and it's all the same anyways. Did you write anything while I was swimming?"

"I started two new poems," she said.

"Will you read them to me?"

"They're not finished."

"I'd like to hear them," he said. He ran his oily hands along her arms, along her side. His fingers curled under, touched her sides, the sides of her breasts.

"Could you get my neck?" she asked.

He did. Her ears too. His hands went back to her sides.

"I'm never going to the lake again," she said.

"Why?" His hands paused.

"I'm reading," she said.

His hands resumed.

"Oh," he said. "Good start."

"I'm never going to the lake again," she said, "because sand is a precursor to glass, and glass is a precursor to those tiny cuts, the kind you get on the palms of your hands, the kind you don't notice until later, when your hands are full of blood. You curve your hands to catch the blood and they only fill faster."

His hands curled around to the sides of her breasts again. He extended his pointer finger on his right hand, fingered the edge of her nipple.

She turned.

"Watch it," she said.

He reached further until he was cupping her breast.

"Watch it," she said again. She rolled over, exposing her breasts for a brief moment before she lifted her top back into place and held it there with her hand. She dropped the book, pushed him away, and stood.

"Sorry," he said.

She clipped her top back on.

"What are you doing?"

"I'm sorry," he said. "I thought…"

She bent and lifted her T-shirt from the ground, slid it back on. Her toes curled and the sand collapsed around them. She felt a tremendous pressure on her chest. She felt angry, uncomfortable. She rolled her shoulders.

"How sorry?" she asked.

"I'm… I don't know, very sorry." He stood up, folded her towel and held it out to her.

She looked at her feet, the sand, at anything but him. She ignored the towel, and he held it out for a moment before hugging it to his chest.

"Sorry enough to eat this?" she asked. She bent and retrieved a handful of sand, held it out to him.

"The sand?"

"Yeah," she said. "Are you willing to eat the sand so I'll forgive you?"

"You want me to eat the sand?"

She nodded. "Before it falls between my fingers."

"How?"

“With your mouth.”

“All of it?”

“As much as you can get down. You have to really try.”

“I’m not going to eat the sand,” he said.

“Then I’m not going to forgive you.”

“But I’m sorry,” he said.

“Prove it.”

“You’re being mean for no reason,” he said.

“For no reason?”

“A handful of sand because I touched a part of your breast?”

“If you eat the handful of sand, you can touch my entire breast. You can hold it.”

“. . .”

"For fifteen seconds."

There were a few other families on the beach by the lake. Small children played in the shallow water. Parents watched from their towels. The day was still.

"In the car?" he asked.

"Wherever," she said.

"Do I have to eat that handful, or can I get my own?"

"You have to eat this handful."

He held out his hands, cupped, pressed together. She held her hand over his palms and spread her fingers.

"Hold your hands together tight," she said. "If any spills, deal's off, and I'll hate you forever."

He was careful to make sure none of the sand spilled. He brought it to his mouth and poured about a quarter of it in. He chewed, swished it around.

"I need water," he coughed. A cloud of sand leapt out, drifted.

“Careful,” she said. “Swallow.”

He swallowed a little. He tried to swallow again, coughed. More sand escaped the open mouth.

“You’re losing sand,” she said.

“Uh cahn hehp it,” he said.

She put her finger to her lips. She rolled up her sleeves. He swallowed a little bit more. He chewed, grimaced, swallowed. There was still a good amount of sand left.

He tried to swallow again but erupted into a coughing fit. He curled his fingers to protect the remaining sand but coughed out cloud after cloud. He choked a little, gargled a little. He bent over, spit into the sand in front of them. He spit clump after clump of sand at his feet.

“I can’t,” he said.

“Fuck you, then,” she said. And she left.

Mary Louise had never hitchhiked before but didn't hesitate to raise her thumb once she'd hit the highway. A truck pulled over almost immediately, about fifty feet ahead of her. The driver was middle-aged and shirtless. He spat little squirts into a Dr. Pepper bottle he stored between his legs. Mary Louise climbed in.

"Where do you want to go?" the driver asked. Mary Louise stared forward. It didn't matter. Away from the lake. Closer to town. She had a few more hours before it was safe to be seen wandering the streets of downtown.

"A few miles that way," she said. She pointed out the windshield. The driver pulled the truck into gear, turned back onto the road. Her swimsuit top was moist with sweat and rubbed a vague shadow into the white T-shirt over it.

"Coming from the lake?" he said. "Did you walk?"

She didn't say anything. Now that she'd had the time to think about it, she didn't think hitchhiking was the best idea. Accepting a ride from this guy was an even worse one.

"Do you like music?" he asked. She didn't respond, so he clicked on the radio. He turned the knob until a soft song fell into place. "Do you like country music?"

Nothing.

"That's okay," he said. He raised the bottle to his lips, squirted. "I didn't always like this kind of thing either. But you slow down after a while, can I say that? Can I offer you a bit of wisdom? I think I can. Or I can speak from experience. You slow down, and slower music starts making sense."

They rode on for another fifteen minutes without speaking. The music played. Song after song, the singers sang about loss and love, how to survive it all or simply that they had.

"You're very pretty," he said.

"This is fine," she said. It was a side of the road much like the one where he'd picked her up. She'd noticed they weren't exactly headed into town, though. She didn't know where they were headed, actually. She'd just pointed, and he'd driven on. There were woods on either side of the road.

He pulled over, turned to her. "Here?"

"Yup." She got out, thanked him.

He watched her walk a bit in the direction from which they came. She turned into the woods, listened for the gravel scrape of his leaving. The car faded on its course. She wiped her eyes, walked deeper into the woods. Mosquitoes grew fat on her arms, the backs of her legs. Specks of mud popped as her sandals lifted. She walked deeper into the woods. She felt guilty of something, but she couldn't say what exactly. The sun was nearly half a day from setting. Skipping school, what had happened between her and her friend, how she'd responded, climbing into a car with a stranger, abandoning that car out of a sudden fear, a sudden correction, too little too late maybe. But none of those reasons seemed the cause. She just didn't feel right. She felt heavy. Each step was a chore. She fought with Gran Joe every so often, over what should be done around the house. The fights didn't last long, though. She would push him, often by simple refusal, until he was just about to boil over, and he would leave the room, the house, the neighborhood. He'd never once yelled at her. Not once in her entire life. She wanted to see it happen.

She could walk back to the road. She could walk deeper into the woods. She had no sense of which would bring her home. The idea of hitchhiking was suddenly repellent. There were three people she could call, her friend, her mother, her Gran Joe. But it wasn't emergency enough yet to call any of them, to make the required admissions.

Night began to fall. The woods shrank around her. Trees were shorter and shorter. Their dry branches curved toward the other trees, mingling with them to form a brittle canopy. The earth cracked, flaked, flung dust at her ankles as she walked. She bent over to avoid the branches, as they grew closer to the ground. The branches reached down, nearly to the earth as she moved deeper into them, but on the other side, there was a lighter shade of blue, things seemed to thin out. She thought she heard the roar of a car every so often, coming from that direction. She was on her hands and knees soon, crawling over the caked earth. The branches snagged her hair, teased it out of the little clips that held it in place. Her sunglasses bounced against her chest. She was on her belly, dragging the lenses in the dust. She remembered the songs she'd heard in the cab of the truck. In one of them, the woman sang, *It ain't no problem, ain't no problem, no problem, the world is spinning. It ain't no problem, the world is spinning.* The gaps between the branches grew smaller. She crawled on her belly toward where the trees seemed to thin, where she would be able to stand, able to walk, able to brush herself off and let her palms sting the cuts along her arms and chest as she approached the road, with its heat waves and oil slicks, only a few feet away, and where she would be so immensely pleased with herself, as her feet met the asphalt like an old friend, and she would begin to walk in whatever direction felt right, while cars passed, and in the distance, she might discern the two waist-high headlights of an approaching truck.

Months passed, years, and the posters faded. Gran Joe posted new ones. He walked with a cane, stapled each new poster individually to billboards, random telephone poles. He turned them in at bookstores, coffee shops, pizza parlors. He called detectives, left messages. Mary Louise's mother ate birthday cakes topped with a variety of ice cream flavors. Mint chocolate chip, strawberry, birthday cake, peppermint, bubble gum, blackberry, rocky road, and plain old vanilla.

She gained weight. She brought home a man who "liked large women." His name was Cliff, and he had only a few teeth. He kept his fingernails long, liked to click them against his glass when he drank.

He'd been a boxer once. He sat on the front porch with Gran Joe and told him the stories of old matches. These conversations were painful for Gran Joe. His entire family had fought with purpose, and this man was doing it for sport. Gran Joe found reasons to leave for a moment, claimed he needed to use the restroom, asked if Cliff needed another beer. Gran Joe sat on the toilet, his pants at his ankles, and did nothing. He enjoyed the time to himself. He wanted to be alone. He wanted Mary Louise back.

When Cliff needed a place to stay, he turned to Mary Louise's mother. Gran Joe suggested the two of them, Cliff and his grandniece, find a place together. She seemed happy around him, or they seemed happy together. She laughed at least. Before, she'd slept most of the time. She'd taken Tylenol PM by the handful, drank Robitussin.

"I'm not saying you've got to leave," he told Mary Louise's mother. "But I can't have him living here."

She left. Their house was a tomb anyway. There were stacks of Missing posters, pictures everywhere of Mary Louise. It would be nice to start over. It would be nice to get out from under all the grief and quiet evenings. Cliff wanted children. He wanted to start a business. He was going to take care of her. Her life could be entirely different.

Cliff mowed lawns for a living. Twenty bucks an hour. He said he met interesting people this way, got to know the neighborhoods and spend most of his days outside. There were worse things he could be doing with his days, he said.

They were able to afford a small apartment on the edge of town. She found work at a 7-Eleven, as the night manager. He mowed during the day, drank during the evenings. She set her alarm an hour early, so they could have sex before he fell asleep and she needed to be at work.

Within three months at their new place, she was pregnant with twins. She named them Joseph and Cliff Jr. the day she found out. She drove home from the gynecologist's office, rubbing her stomach, singing to herself. *Not to myself*, she thought, *to Joseph and Cliff Jr.* She couldn't be happier that there would be two. They could watch out for each other and neither would ever get lost.

Cliff broke a lamp when he found out. He was shirtless and yelling and circling the open space in the living room. They didn't have money for two kids. He pushed her, pressed her against a wall.

"What am I supposed to do?" he said.

She couldn't breathe, not really. She couldn't say anything.

"Well?"

She thought to knee him in the groin. She thought to hit him in the mouth, claw out his eyes, hit him in the gut. She thought of choking him, stabbing him, drowning him in the puddle behind their apartment complex, thick with mosquito eggs.

She shook her head, looked around the room. She didn't fight. She gave in, went limp in his arms. He stepped back and she stuttered forward, regained her balance.

"I'm sorry," he said. He left the room, got a beer from the fridge, and sat down at the table.

Her blood was still hot. Her body was sore all over. While he drank, she found the gun he kept in his closet, a twenty-two he'd stolen from a neighbor's yard, years before.

"Right off the porch," he liked to say.

The television exploded and he was up and out of his seat. Beer spilled onto his legs and splashed against his bare chest.

"What the hell?"

He entered the living room, and she had the gun against her collarbone, smoke at the barrel. The television spat a spark. She turned the gun on him, asked him to leave.

"That's my gun," he said.

"It was never your gun," she said.

She wrote Gran Joe for money. He sent checks, along with letters asking her to visit, asking if he could. She answered his letters, but never his questions. She talked about other things. She talked about work, about her body, what it was like, having two inside you instead of one. She didn't always send these letters. They were personal, and Gran Joe had never liked hearing about that kind of thing. He didn't push the issue of a visit, asked every few letters how she might feel about the idea. And she never replied.

She was starting over. This was something new. Cliff didn't matter, he never had. She changed Cliff Jr.'s name to Jimmi. Jimmi and Joseph. She liked the sound of that, for a set of twins.

She couldn't get comfortable in the apartment she'd shared with Cliff. It wasn't the right space to raise a set of boys, and she couldn't shake the feeling that Cliff was still there, in another room somewhere, on the toilet, drinking in the kitchen, behind the shower curtain. She found a carriage-house apartment behind the home of an old couple, married fifty-two years. They left her alone mostly, congratulated her on the boys. Every so often, the wife from the couple would bring her some of whatever they were having, a few slices of chicken in gravy, some mashed potatoes, some apple crisp. But she refused the food more often than not. She felt strong, like she was doing a good thing. The right thing. Her sons grew inside her. The checks from Gran Joe came biweekly. She worked at the 7-Eleven until she was seven months. Then she started accepting food whenever her landlord made the offer. It wasn't long before they offered to have her in. She ate with them at their small dinner table, in the middle of the kitchen. They sat back together, after the meal, considered one another. She felt like she filled the entire room. She imagined herself befriending them. She imagined their always wishing they'd had a daughter, seeing her as such. They would bring her into their house, feed her, love her, and when they died, they would leave her everything.

She imagined the old woman dying. The husband so stricken with grief that he asked her in for dinner, time and time again.

"You're very beautiful," he would say. "You are very, very beautiful."

At first, she would care for him. Feed him, keep his medications straight, cook, clean, that kind of thing. He would grow to depend on her, to love her, and he would ask her to marry him, and she would say yes because when he died, he would leave her everything.

"Thank you," she said.

They nodded.

"We like to watch a movie after dinner," the old man said. "Or sometimes the TV. Would you like to join us?"

"Henry," said his wife. "She wants to sleep."

"Of course," said the man. "Forgive me." He took their plates.

"This was lovely," she said.

"Yes," said the old woman. She rose and went to the counter. She stood there for a moment, her hands hovering at the linoleum, then left for the living room. The television clicked on. The room filled with laughter.

The old man had his back to his tenant at the table. He wiped the plates with a flower print rag.

"Good night," she said.

He nodded. "Good night."

She applied to be a part of a program that would pay for her hospital bills when she had Jimmi and Joseph. She had to sign a paper that said she had no way of supporting herself, and never would.

The babies came. She was relieved. For a day or two, she was relieved. Then she started working out. She jumped rope in the center of the carriage house while the babies slept. She worked extra hours. Her landlords babysat a handful of times.

She got money from the state. She worked. She put ads in the paper, online. She was looking for someone independent, with a comfortable living situation. She was looking for someone who was mature. Someone who knew what wine went with what. Someone who worked out. Someone who liked mothers. Someone with money. She was looking for someone with money.

She placed a T-shirt over the lap of one of the sleeping babies. She touched the nose of the other, his cheek.

"Jimmi," she said, pointing to the shirt. "That's *your* name."

He did not move when she tucked it between his legs and the car seat. The face of Jimi Hendrix moaned up at her.

"And Joe," she said. She followed the same procedure with the other child, securing the edges of a Joe Perry shirt between his limbs and the cushion of the car seat.

She got home early. There wasn't a soul on the road.

The babies slept on while she prepared dinner. The carrot skins slid off easily, with only a few strokes. The water boiled after only a moment. She had a small glass of wine. A strand of pasta stuck to the wall.

Perry arrived. He saw the babies, swaddled in the Jimi Hendrix T-shirt and the Joe Perry shirt, and he put on a record. She danced into the room, a second glass of wine in her hand.

"I made pasta," she said.

They made love on the living room floor. She scuffed her knees on the carpet. Jimmi stirred. The pasta cooled. She told Perry not to stop when he was ready to come, not to slow down. He didn't. After, he slid down between her knees and she leaned over him, pressed her palms into the carpet. She made quiet sounds: the baby was only a few feet away. She glanced every now and then at the babies, checked to make sure they were sleeping, safe, as something moved through her, a scream of blood rounded the curves of each ear and her body seized, released, and Perry paused.

"Did you?"

She slapped the carpet, and he began to move again, his fingers, his tongue, his chin. He pressed her with the tip of his nose.

Joe stirred. She looked over once more, before she collapsed.

They lay together on the carpet, slick and smiling.

"Will that fuck him up?" Perry asked. He meant either.

She shrugged. She didn't think so. Their eyes had been closed the entire time; they'd held them tight, there in their chairs.

She and Perry ate the pasta naked. She dropped noodles onto her lap, between her legs and onto the chair.

"We need a dog," she said.

They bought a dog for the babies, named it Sid.

"Sid's your dog," she explained.

Joe cupped his hands, held them up. Jimmi coughed some foam onto his lips, sucked it back in.

"One day you won't be able to imagine having lived without him. That's the way I feel about you."

Jimmi coughed again, a mess of white foam onto his cheeks, neck, and chest. She wiped it away with the hem of her shirt.

Joe and Jimmi grew up alongside Sid. Sid was big and black and the toddlers could ride him a few steps before sliding off. Perry held each of them, one at a time, on Sid's back until they slid, and Perry cried, "Lift off!" and flew the toddler around the room in sweeping arcs and curves until bringing him down safely to land on the couch by his brother.

As a young boy, Jimmi spent a lot of time by the creek behind their house. He caught lizards and snakes and reptiles and showed them to Sid, who was almost always with him. Joe lost interest in Sid early on. When he pushed at Joe's legs at the table, Joe swatted at him, and Jimmi told him to stop. Jimmi fed the dog bites of food with one hand, held his own bites with the other.

When Jimmi caught animals, he brought them home to show his mother and her boyfriend. Perry didn't live with them, but he was around all of the time. Perry had his own house. He drove a nice car that went faster than Jimmi was comfortable going. He didn't like riding with Perry in the car because Perry would rev the engine. He would say, "Listen to her, she wants it," and he would speed through lights, take corners too fast, and curse at the other drivers when they got in his way.

Sometimes Jimmi kept the animals he found. Most of the time, he let them go. His mother always made him choose his favorite one. He could keep that one for a week before letting it go. He had two frogs and one grass snake in his permanent collection. They had not left the porch when he placed them there after a week of taking care of them at home.

"They're spoiled," Perry had said.

"They love me," Jimmi had said.

"I'm sure they do. But I bet they also love their freedom."

When they were still there in the morning, Jimmi said, "They love me more than their freedom, Mom." And that was that. Jimmi became the proud owner of each brand-new pet.

Sid was always hungry. He slobbered on the carpet, on the porch, on Jimmi. Sid dipped his face into the creek, hung his cheeks just below the water as if to clean them. He watched the small fish with a keen eye. He did not pounce. He had never really pounced. He behaved as if he were born trained. He had sat and watched the two frogs and the grass snake on the porch. He cocked his head. They didn't move. There seemed an understanding between them. Jimmi said they were all his friends, and his friends would not hurt one another.

It was summer. The heat was getting worse and worse. Their backyard was without trees, without shade, so they started keeping Sid in the house. One day, while Jimmi and Joe were at school, their mother at work, Sid knocked the cage containing the two frogs and the grass snake off the bookcase. It fell, at least. Perry discovered the mess, blamed the dog, but Jimmi insisted they had no way of knowing what really happened. The frogs and the grass snake were gone, though. The tank lay shattered on the carpet in Joe and Jimmi's room, a splatter of dark brown where the water had soaked in. Crickets leapt around the room, under the doors and into the kitchen.

"You have to clean it up," Joe said. He turned on the television, opened a math book at his lap. He set down his pencil.

Jimmi brought Sid outside. He looked him in his eyes. Sid's mouth ran. Saliva streamed from his sagging cheeks. He would not look at Jimmi. He would not sit still.

Jimmi gripped the collar and forced Sid to look at him.

"Did you eat the frogs and the snake?"

Sid couldn't answer. He didn't understand the question. Jimmi could tell just by looking at him. Why were dogs so stupid?

"Why are dogs so stupid?"

Jimmi's mother was drinking wine and leafing through a magazine at the kitchen table.

"They don't have access to the same opportunities as you," she said. "Oh." She put her hand to her mouth, looked around the room for someone who could appreciate her joke.

"Sid's a stupid dog," Jimmi said. "I think he was born stupid. I think I hate stupid dogs."

"Sid's not stupid, sweetie," she said. "He's just a dog, and dogs don't think like humans think. He might be very smart for a dog."

"He's an idiot," Jimmi said. He kicked the kitchen wall and left the room. He walked past the broom Joe had set out for him in the hall, over the glass on the floor in his bedroom, and climbed into bed.

In the morning, Jimmi woke up earlier than his mother or brother. He went out back, where they had chained Sid. He unclipped Sid's collar from the lead. He unhitched the back fence, opened it wide. There was a field behind the house. It led down to the creek he liked to explore. The creek he used to explore with Sid.

"Go," he said.

Sid sat.

"Get," Jimmi said.

The dog collapsed onto his paws. His tongue fell out. It was slick and shining and foamy.

"You're the worst dog ever," Jimmi said.

Sid slobbered onto the grass. Then he ate the slobber and the grass. Jimmi went inside and got a plate of leftovers from the fridge. He placed it on the other side of the fence.

"Eat," he said. "Eat this."

The dog got up. He went over to Jimmi, sniffed his hands,

licked them, then lowered his head to the plate. Jimmi closed the fence and hitched it. He had to push Sid's butt slightly to get the fence fully closed. The dog had looked up, but only for a moment. He went back to eating. It was spinach quiche, marbled with thick streams of green. Jimmi knew Sid would like it.

"Have you seen Sid?" his mother asked, later that morning.

"Nope," said Jimmi.

Perry hung a few signs on telephone poles around town: Missing Lab. But they heard nothing. Jimmi told his mother he asked people on the street, told them he'd gone to the grocery stores, to the neighbors. No one knew anything.

After a month of searching, they had a mock funeral in the backyard. Perry dug a hole, where he placed what was left of the dog food. He said it seemed like a waste. Jimmi's mother was openly weeping. Joe dug his toe into the dirt at his feet. He looked around. They gathered together around the hole. Had a moment of silence. They watched two movies that night. A cartoon, and an action movie Perry had chosen. In it, a detective found his girlfriend's dog skinned and hung from a doorframe in his apartment. Perry laughed a little, which made Joe laugh hysterically.

"Quit it," said his mother.

Jimmi ate a handful of popcorn. He felt sad, but guessed he knew why they were laughing. The dead dog looked really fake. The detective was overacting. None of it seemed very real. His heart was racing. He ate another handful of popcorn.

No one wanted another dog. Sid had been their dog, and Sid was gone. Jimmi collected more snakes. He convinced his parents to let him keep them a little longer than a week sometimes. His room smelled like dead crickets and feces. Joe complained, lit candles. He demanded his own room and, eventually, their mother cleared her study of the boxes of photos and keepsakes she'd been storing there since she'd met Perry, since he'd moved them into this new home, an actual house, with actual rooms and two bathrooms, and their family had filled the extra space like a goldfish.

They grew up. All of Jimmi's frogs and most of the snakes died. One lived for ten years, until Jimmi and Joe started high school. It died one winter—Joe had unplugged the heat rock to make room for a guitar amp—and that was the last of the snakes.

Jimmi's mother was dressed in lace. It was the first time she had ever been entirely so. She looked elegant. She felt important, well-shaped, soft, and worth touching. She felt like many people would want to touch her. Perry watched her from the bed. She fiddled with powders at the chest of drawers. They were new, and so was the lace. Perry bought her new things. They had no more money than before, but they were beginning to look as if they did. She was losing weight. She felt happier than she'd been for as long as she could remember. Her sons were growing up to be mature young men. She felt proud of the three of them, proud of what they'd accomplished. They were normal. That meant they had less to worry about in general. Life was stressful but they did not have the added anxiety of an insecure position in the world. Perry worked. She worked too. Perry unbuttoned his pants, slid them down to his knees. His wife raised her head, but did not look over. She dabbed at her neck with a small brush, streaked a thick line of white powder, which she smoothed with her hand. He moved his hand along his thighs and watched her.

"Thank you," she said. She did not look away from the mirror.

With the palm of his hand, he encouraged his penis to lift.

“These.” She pressed her lips together. “Are fantastic.”

He curled his fingers.

“Come to bed,” he said.

She turned to him, smiled.

“In a minute.”

Joe and Jimmi were athletic, muscular, likeable. They did well in school. They were popular. People were attracted to them. Both men and women were drawn to them. People seemed to feel better around them, comfortable. The hallways brightened with their presence. Joe embraced this. He developed an enormous circle of friends. He knew nearly everyone in the school, in their hometown. People waved to him on the street. Jimmi kept to himself mostly. He was quiet, withdrawn, but he was still magnetic.

Jimmi had one close friend. He was small, bony. The friend admired Jimmi. He said yes to nearly everything Jimmi suggested. They ran together, explored together. They threw bricks through the windows at the Piggly Wiggly. They slashed the tires of strangers. They snuck into their neighbors' backyards, swam in their pools.

Jimmi went to the creek with his friend, threw trash from the creek bed into the water. He threw in a McDonald's cup. He threw in a chunk of metal.

"Do your parents still fuck?" Jimmi asked.

"Yeah," said his friend.

"How do you know?"

"I don't know. I can just tell. I think I've heard them."

His friend threw a Doritos bag. It was lifted by the wind, curled on a current, and then it landed back on the creek bed where they stood, only a few feet away.

"What did it sound like?"

Jimmi gathered a handful of rocks and went over to the bag. He dropped them in.

"Like a giraffe," he said. "Like a giraffe, I think. And maybe a dog or something. Like animals trying to move the furniture."

"Sick."

Jimmi threw the weighted Doritos bag at the water. It hit the surface with a smack. It sank. Bubbles rose to the surface and broke.

"Nice," said his friend.

Jimmi shrugged.

"You guys have nice furniture," he said, after a moment.

Jimmi shrugged again. There was very little garbage left where they were standing. Strips of plastic, paper adhered to rock. Nothing he could throw. Nothing that would sink.

"Does your dad have a big dick?" Jimmi said.

"I don't know."

"I bet he does," Jimmi said. "I bet he has a big dick."

Jimmi's friend said he didn't know. Jimmi's friend had only seen two dicks in real life. His and his father's. He had no way of knowing how either of them compared to the rest of the dicks in the world. He had no idea what was normal.

"Okay," Jimmi said. He lowered his pants. He spread his legs and swayed at his hips. "Ooh," he said. He pulled up his pants, threw a plastic bottle into the creek.

"Yeah," his friend said. "I think you're right. I think my dad has a huge dick."

While they thought Jimmi was at the creek, Perry went down on his mother at the kitchen table. They had been drinking lemonade and he'd slid under the table like a lithe teenager. He parted her knees, pulled her underwear aside. She settled into her seat. She put down her glass and it clicked on the table.

She admired her children. How intensely they felt things. How dedicated and focused they could be. How they embraced their wants, their interests in a way that had seemed foreign to her for many years.

Jimmi's mother gripped her seat to steady herself. Perry was on his knees, focused, working, rhythmic, determined. She kept her eyes on the window. She closed them. She felt guilty, didn't know why. Condensation from the glass pearled along its side, grew heavy and fell. A ring gathered on the table. Her rings clicked the chair she held. Perry's neck cracked and she rose up slightly. He was growing a beard. She could feel it on her inner thigh. It tickled. It did not seem connected to him. Her rings clicked and she watched the window. A cluster of cicadas detonated, and she felt the blood inside of her, moving through her. Perry slowed.

"Did you?" he said.

She shook her chin, closed her eyes. He slid back under the table. Jimmi was at the backdoor, his face pressed against the window. He saw his mother squirm. Her eyes were closed. He knew what was happening, but he did not know what was happening. He told his friend to go home, sat on the step at the door for what felt like hours. He pressed a beetle with his fingertip, popped it against the hot concrete.

"Are you having another baby?"

Jimmi found his mother on the couch, considering a basket full of laundry. She looked up.

"No." She cocked her head. "I don't think so."

"Good." Jimmi came around and sat on the couch with her, on the far side of the laundry basket.

"Why?"

"I don't think you should," he said.

"Why's that?"

"Babies are awful," he said. "They wet themselves. They cry. They can't do anything for themselves."

"You were a wonderful baby," she said. "I don't even remember you crying. I'm sure you did, but I don't remember it."

"Joe did all the crying?"

"Joe didn't cry either. You were both perfect babies," she said.

"Just don't have another baby, okay?"

"We won't," she said.

He didn't like the way she said *we*, like it was her and Perry against him.

"We won't anytime soon. But a baby would be a wonderful thing, Jimmi. Not a bad thing."

"It would be a pink wriggling thing that would pee and not take care of itself and be disgusting. They're disgusting, Mom."

"We—"

Jimmi knocked the basket of laundry onto the floor. Some fell out, but most clung to the bundle she'd made when pulling it all from the dryer.

"Jimmi," she said.

"Don't, okay?"

"Jimmi."

He left the room, kicked a small pile of socks. It tumbled once or twice then settled. She gathered the laundry back into the basket and brought it into the kitchen where Perry was drinking lemonade and reading the paper.

"What was that?" Perry said.

"He knocked the laundry over."

"That's it?"

"He said we shouldn't have another baby."

Perry smiled. "Smart kid."

One Sunday, Jimmi and his friend were checking dumpsters behind the Kmart.

"What are we looking for?" asked his friend.

"People drop babies in these things. We're looking for babies," Jimmi said.

"Gross." His friend lowered the lid of one dumpster, opened the next. "This one's full of books."

“What kind?”

“Says, ‘The Gateway to Lucid Dreams.’” Jimmi’s friend held up one of the coverless books.

“Found it.” Jimmi propped the plastic lid of the dumpster up with on hand, reached into its open mouth with the other. He pulled out a slick body, roughly the length of his forearm.

“Gross!” Jimmi’s friend dropped the book. “Is it…?”

“A baby,” Jimmi said. “Someone left it here.”

It was an opossum, a few days dead. Jimmi wrapped it in newspaper from the garbage. He carried it under his arm as they walked home.

“Let’s throw it at a car,” said his friend.

“Can’t throw a baby at a car,” Jimmi said. “We need to give it a proper burial.”

His friend nodded.

“Let’s throw it into the river,” he said. “From the bridge. Let’s put it on the railroad tracks."

When Jimmi and his friend got home, the front door was locked. No one answered when Jimmi knocked. Joe was out, he ran on Sundays, spent the rest of the day with his running friends and those that flocked to them as the day dragged on. Jimmi went around to the back of the house, the opossum under his arm. He stood on the AC unit at the side of the house, cracked one of his bedroom windows. He had long ago removed the screen for easy access. He slid through the window and lowered himself onto his desk. The opossum slid back and forth in the moist fold of his armpit. He felt its skin give to the pressure, glide, along with the muscle, against the bone.

"Let me in," said Jimmi's friend, from the window.

Jimmi opened his bedroom door and stepped into the hallway slowly, cautiously, the opossum sliding out from under his arm and behind him. Its tail worked its way out of the mouth of the bag, dangled there like the tiny tip of an off-white tongue.

His mother was on the living room floor. Perry was pushing her forward from behind. She was entirely nude. Perry, from the waist down. He had on a black T-shirt. Jimmi hurled the opossum, and it struck the far window, bounced with a thud, and landed on the carpet beside them.

His mother fell onto her front. Perry lay upon her.

"Give us a moment," his mother said.

"What is that?" Perry pulled himself up. He stood over the opossum, his wet, erect penis glistening in the sun that leaked through the cracks in the mini blinds.

Jimmi's mother covered her face with hands.

"We need a moment, Jimmi," his mother said.

Jimmi's friend tapped the window.

His mother reached for a cushion from the couch. Her fingers fell shy of its edge, fell to the carpet.

Perry stood over the opossum, looked back at Jimmi.

"What the fuck is this? What are you trying to pull here?" He brought his foot up over the opossum, pressed it down upon the rotten animal's bulging stomach. It popped, slung sludge onto the carpet, Perry's ankles. His calves were dotted with the mess. He turned his body, his glistening dick, toward Jimmi. "Well?"

"I'm sorry," Jimmi said.

"Sorry?" Perry brought his foot out of the dead rodent. He stepped toward Jimmi, tracking the sludge along the carpet as he did so. Jimmi stepped back. "Sorry for what?"

"Stop it, Perry." Jimmi's mother was pulling her clothes from a chair by the couch. She pulled on her shirt, her pants. She rubbed her hands against her head, pressed her hair down. "Stop."

"What's he sorry for?" Perry turned toward her. "What were you trying to do?"

"I... I don't know. You have to leave," Jimmi said.

"This is my house, Jimmi. You're a guest."

Perry was only a foot or so away from him now. Jimmi thought he could feel the heat of his body.

"Perry, get dressed. Let's talk about this."

"You're a spoiled shit," Perry said. He grabbed Jimmi's wrist and squeezed the veins just beneath his palm.

Jimmi resisted, tried to pull his arm away, but Perry held strong, stared him in his eyes.

Jimmi hit him. He hit him once across the mouth. Once against the back of his head.

"Jimmi."

Perry fell and Jimmi turned around, ran back to his room. His friend was still tapping at the window.

"Jimmi," he said. "What's going on?"

Jimmi exited through his bedroom window, climbed down the AC unit and past his friend, who followed him asking what had happened to the baby.

Jimmi led him to the creek. He took his shirt off, his shorts. He looked at his friend who asked again what had happened.

Jimmi climbed into the creek.

"You and I are going to get married," he told his friend. "We're going to be a new family."

Jimmi's friend just stared back at him. Jimmi was near nude, ankle deep in the creek. He stared at his friend like a bull. His friend removed his shirt, his shorts. He climbed into the creek, ankle deep.

They both waited a moment. The water broke against their ankles, moved past them. Jimmi took his friend's wrists.

"There," he said. "It's done."

When they came back later that evening, Perry was gone. Jimmi's mother was gone. Joe was in the living room with two girls, a blonde and brunette. Jimmi told them he was leaving, moving in with his friend.

"You're doing what?" Joe said.

"I'm leaving. Alex and I are moving in together. Tell Mom we got married. Tell her, her gay son got married and is running off with his husband to go live anywhere other than here."

Jimmi threw a few shirts in a bag, some underwear. He didn't know what to bring. He didn't want to think about it. They weren't sure where they were going. It didn't matter.

"I didn't know you were gay," said Joe.

"Yeah, well."

And Jimmi left.

Jimmi and Alex drove late into the night. They stopped for gas. Jimmi bought cigarettes. They kept driving.

"What are we looking for?" Alex said.

Jimmi smoked.

"I didn't know you smoked."

"Yeah," Jimmi said. "Turn here."

Alex turned. He followed Jimmi's directions until they reached Oak Street, where Jimmi told him to stop alongside a dark blue Mustang convertible. Jimmi got out of the car.

"Pop the trunk," he said.

Jimmi came out from behind the car, tire iron in hand, and struck the headlights of the convertible. He struck the hood. He shattered the windshield, each window. He popped the taillights, dented the hood.

The alarm rang out. He struck the doors, the hood once more. He got back into Alex's car. They drove until sunrise. Alex talked. Jimmi smoked.

"That felt good," Jimmi said.

He kissed Alex. And after that, Alex wanted to hold his hand. Jimmi fiddled with the locks. He smoked. He changed the radio station, kept his hands busy.

"I need to stop at my house," Alex said. "I… I need to tell my parents I'm alright. We've been gone a long time."

"We can't do that," Jimmi said.

"But I've never been gone this long."

"One night?"

Alex shook his head. He tried to touch Jimmi's hand again.

"Whatever, I'm staying in the car," said Jimmi.

Perry was waiting for them at Alex's house. His Mustang was there, its bumper dangling from the front like a loose tooth.

He pulled Jimmi out of the car, dropped him in the street. He sat on his back, pressed his face into the asphalt and held it there. He turned it back and forth against the road.

"What the fuck are you doing?" Perry said, over and over again. "What the fuck are you doing, Jimmi?"

Alex hit him on the back of the head and Perry rose up. Alex shrank. Jimmi hit Perry again in the back of the head. He hit him in the face, in the stomach, in the ear. He pushed him and Perry collapsed. Jimmi grabbed Perry's hair and wriggled his face over and against the curb, tried to feel for the click of his teeth against the concrete. He brought his foot down.

"Ha!" He exhaled for strength, and to cover up the sound of Perry's face cracking.

It wasn't long before the police arrived. Jimmi and Alex ran but were caught only a few blocks over. They were arrested together. Alex insisted he'd been a part of it, but Jimmi assured them he had not. He'd done nothing. He was only trying to help his friend. Jimmi was tried and convicted for manslaughter, sentenced to twenty-five years. He was eighteen when he went in.

Alex visited him monthly for the first three years. Joe never once visited. He wrote a letter stating he thought Jimmi needed the time to himself.

As much as I love you, the letter read, *I know, and I know you know, that you deserve this. Life is invaluable, Jimmi. You know that. You've always known that. Remember your snakes? Your frogs? Remember when we were only kids and you managed to get that piece of glass out of my mouth before I cut myself? Remember crying because I was crying because I thought you were trying to hurt me? You were trying to save me. You did save me. Remember that? Remember that, Jimmi, while you're away. I love you.*

Their mother delivered the letter. She could hardly stop crying long enough to speak, long enough to say it was from his brother. She was convinced their family was cursed. She told Jimmi it wasn't his fault. They'd been cursed from the beginning. Their entire bloodline, for years, and for something that had happened so long ago no one could remember what it was, so they would remain cursed forever. Jimmi asked her not to visit anymore. She upset him. He didn't want to see her. He needed to believe things would get better. He needed to believe it wasn't over.

"Don't visit me anymore," he said. "Tell Alex the same."

Alex didn't listen. Not at first. When he got sick, he wasn't able to come as much as he would have liked. Eventually, he was hospitalized. Cancer in his marrow. He had only a few months.

Jimmi met his wife through a letters-to-convicts service, which he enrolled in after fifteen years of incarceration. She asked him about life in prison, about what he'd been like before he went inside. He told her he hadn't known what he wanted. He'd been confused. Things hadn't been easy. Not knowing what he wanted had left him feeling helpless, without guidance or clarity. But that had all changed once he began to lose things. Once he lost his freedom, lost his best friend, his right to a normal life, he knew what he wanted. He wanted those things. He wanted friendship, love, television, cold beers. He wanted people he could rely on. He wanted people who could rely on him. He wanted children, a wife. He wanted to devote himself to something. He wanted to show God he was worth loving. He wanted to be worth loving. When he was finally released, they were married. She was pregnant within a year. They were happy together, though Jimmi was given to fits of melancholy. He put holes in the walls, but never raised his hands to her. He was holding her hand when the baby came.

"She's beautiful," he told his wife. She couldn't hear him. She'd gone still only a few moments after Clara had appeared. "She's perfect," Jimmi said.

When their mother died, Jimmi flew home, to help his brother with the arrangements.

Joseph had a home in their old neighborhood where he lived with his wife and two daughters. Jimmi and his daughter roomed with Joe for a week while they finalized the details concerning their mother's burial. She was buried on a Sunday, in the morning.

After the funeral, Jimmi's daughter, Clara, asked if his mother and her mother were together now because they had both died. Jimmi said they were. She asked if we all had to die and if he, Dad, was going to die too and Jimmi said, yes, they were all going to die. He was going to die too. But not for a long time, and it wasn't something to be afraid of. She asked why not? Why not be afraid? And he said because life was a very, very, very good thing, and death was a part of it, just like any other part.

"What do you do when a part is scary?" she asked.

"Refocus your attention," he said. "Think of something else."

Clara said that, okay, she wasn't afraid, but it made her sad, and Jimmi said that was fine, it made him sad too.

He and Joe spent only a small amount of that week alone together. Joe told a few jokes. Jimmi drank cup after cup of coffee.

"How's Clara?" Joe asked.

"She's good," said Jimmi.

"How are you?" he asked.

"I'm good," said Jimmi.

On the plane ride home, Clara closed her eyes during takeoff and landing.

"I thought you weren't afraid," said Jimmi.

"I'm not," said his daughter, "I'm thinking of something else." Jimmi read his daughter bedtime stories and the girl sometimes described what she saw.

They were in a two-story apartment, the monkey and the man. Their hands were rounded and still, but still able to grip onto things like ladder rungs, which they needed to climb to the second story. The monkey liked records and the man liked CDs. When they weren't on adventures, they did things like climb into a car with their friends and drive to the Great Wall of China. These were fairly quiet trips, fairly normal. Nothing much happened, but they took lots of pictures, and told the stories over and over.

Jimmi's daughter loved preschool. She loved playing with the other kids. She started telling stories all the time to anyone who would listen. She told stories about things she'd heard other people talk about, and filled in what she didn't know.

"My dad hit a squirrel with his car today. Its body was stiff, but his face was smooshed. He got out of the car and picked the squirrel up off the ground and wrapped it in a shirt he'd just picked up from the cleaners. The shirt was so white he could see the squirrel leaking through it, so he put the squirrel and the shirt in the backseat and drove us all home where he buried the squirrel in the shirt in the backyard. He told me it was a nice shirt, and the squirrel would like to be buried with it. I said the squirrel would like to be buried with a nut, or in a nut. A nut he could eat himself out of. My dad said next time, and I said what?, because I wanted him to say it again, and he said *never mind.*"

"You told that story at school?" Jimmi asked.

Clara nodded.

"Did you get in trouble?"

She shook her head.

"Cool," Jimmi said. He wrote the story down and put it on the refrigerator.

In the park, Jimmi talked to the other parents. The mothers, the fathers, the children now and then. Clara and the other kids built an enormous sandcastle and disappeared inside of it. The children came out hours later—Jimmi and the other parents were on the bench, patiently waiting—and they looked entirely exhausted. A little older, a little surer of themselves. There was sand in their pockets, in their hair. They weren't able to describe what they'd done, what they'd seen exactly. But they took deep breaths and left with their parents, hand in hand, and none of them were much like they had been before.

Clara asked Jimmi when he was going to find another wife. But Jimmi didn't want to focus on that, on himself. He wanted to raise his daughter to the best of his abilities, and he would seek out someone when the time was right.

Clara was less social in grade school. She had two best friends, Sam and Susie. They were over every weekend, made forts out of the couch cushions. They draped a canopy roof of bed sheets over the cushions and sat beneath them in the darkness together. They ate bowls of chips and told stories under the canopy. Sam was in love with Clara, anyone could have seen it. Around her, he was red-faced most of the time. He was comfortable but looked to her for approval for nearly every decision.

"We could angle this pillow, extend this area and make a little kitchen space where we can keep the bag of chips and the crackers, right Clara?"

When they weren't hidden in the fort, Jimmi watched the kid flirt with his daughter, watched him pine away for her, and realized things would get very complicated as she grew up.

One Sunday, Sam asked Jimmi for permission to dig a hole. Clara was in the backyard, and Jimmi was moving about the house, doing Sunday things, checking occasionally on Clara in the yard whenever his fluttering led him from one room to another. Sam knocked and Jimmi came to the door.

"I was thinking of digging a hole," the boy said, "for Clara."

"Okay," Jimmi said. "Do you think that's something she'd like?"

"I don't know," the boy said. "I'm not sure what I'd find."

"You're looking for something?"

"Not exactly."

"What's the use of the hole?"

"It's for Clara," said the boy.

"Right," said Jimmi.

"I would need to borrow your shovel," the boy said. "My

parents say they're particular about their tools."

"What if I'm particular about my tools?" asked Jimmi.

"Are you?"

Jimmi thought a moment. He was most interested in what exactly this kid meant. How far would the hole go? What would they use it for? *Where* would it go? What was the point, exactly?

"Where are you going to dig?" Jimmi asked.

"I haven't decided yet."

"Shovel's in the back," Jimmi said. He led the boy through the house, to the backyard. They got the shovel from the garage. Clara waved, started to come over. Sam took the shovel and left.

"Was that Sam?" she asked.

"It was," her father said.

"Did he want to play?"

"He wanted to borrow the shovel."

"Why?"

"To dig."

"Dig what?" she asked.

"I'm not entirely sure," Jimmi said.

The next day Sam began to dig. He wandered deep into the woods. He found a circular clearing and dug in its center. He dug for hours, until he tired, then he rested. He drank water from one of the many bottles he'd brought with him. He went home just after dark and went back after school the next day. He isolated himself more or less, and his friends began to wonder. His parents wondered less, they assumed he was with his friends.

The hole got deeper. The hole got very deep.

One day, Susie and Clara decided to follow him. After

school, he left the building and headed home. He entered his garage, came out a moment later with the shovel in hand. He walked, the shovel's head hanging down, scraping a line in the pavement behind him, until he abandoned the sidewalk for the tall grass. They hung back, watched from behind buildings and houses, bushes and cars. He trailed through the tall grass until he reached the edge of the woods, and he entered them without hesitation. They followed, a little more closely now, less sure of his path, less confident of their ability to anticipate his movement. They turned flat behind trees, they moved on their heels, lightly on the tips of their toes, until finally they reached the clearing. There was a small lamp there, a chair, bottles of water, a basket, and an enormous dark hole. Beside the hole was a raised wheel with a cord of rope dangling from either side, into the hole. Sam lifted the lantern and walked to the edge of the hole. He crouched and turned, dropped his legs over the edge and disappeared. They waited a moment, a few minutes. They looked at one another. They moved to the hole's edge.

When they looked over, there was only darkness. They could see nothing but the rounded curve of the hole's edge, the dark dirt disappearing. There was no light. Nothing but the two ropes dangling from the wheel and a thin rope ladder hung from the hole's rim, the cords soiled and frayed with use.

They climbed into the hole, Susie after Clara. They lowered themselves slowly, rung after rung. They heard the faint, chunky sounds of Sam digging. Susie did not look down. Clara looked over her shoulder, past her feet, and saw a bit of glitter somewhere in the distance. It moved. It bounced. It turned this way and that, as if alarmed at their approach. Sam set the lantern down, and the light seemed to grow around him.

Sam dug steadily, patiently, dropped the dirt into a bucket at his feet. When the bucket was full, his tired arms gripped the rope that was tied to its handle. He pulled. The bucket lifted. He pulled until the bucket lifted out of sight. He tied the rope to a large white rock they had not noticed before, and he turned toward the rope ladder.

"Hi Sam," Clara said.

Sam hadn't planned to wait this long before telling his friends about the hole, before showing Clara and explaining it had all been for her. But once he started, he'd been unable to stop. He devised new plans to keep the project going, the rock and pulley for excavating loose dirt, for example. There was always more hole to be dug, he realized, so he kept going.

"Why did you start?" Clara asked. They were sitting around the hole's edge. Sam's feet dangled above the darkness. Clara and Susie sat a few feet back.

Sam looked at the hole for a moment. He looked at Clara.

"Why did I start?"

She nodded. It was twilight. Her pale skin had a bluish hue. Her dark hair looked even darker, nearly black. She wiped her mouth with her wrist.

He shrugged, looked back to the hole.

"Can we help?" asked Susie.

Sam dug and Susie pulled the rope that brought the bucket of dirt up to Clara who carried the bucket off into the woods, where she distributed the contents onto the rising layer of topsoil.

They went on like this for days. They angled the hole, so it eventually ran parallel to the earth above it. Susie snuck a shovel and bucket out of her parents' garage and brought them to the dig site. She dug alongside Sam, filled her own bucket as she did. Clara retrieved two buckets at a time, carried them one after the other, out into the woods.

They kept this up for days. They came home covered in mud and cuts and fell almost immediately asleep.

"Where have you kids been going?" asked Jimmi.

They were at the breakfast table. Clara had a scrape on her cheek from the night before. It was swollen, discolored. The bucket's dirty handle had slipped from her hand, and she'd lost her balance, fell against the bucket's edge.

"Just playing in the woods," she said. She ate eggs on bread with bacon and cheese. She mopped up the extra yolk with her crust.

"Does this have to do with why Sam borrowed my shovel?"

Clara thought a moment. She hadn't thought of that bizarre exchange for some time—it seemed somehow unreal.

"Yes," she said. "I guess it does."

"This is impressive," Jimmi said. They'd dug an impressive hole. They'd tunneled into the earth. They had a system. Jimmi bought a few more shovels, told them to invite their friends. Soon they had a team of thirty plus. A long line of diggers and excavators with Sam at the front and Clara at the back. The air was thin at the front of the tunnel, so every now and then Clara, who stood at the edge of the hole, opened her mouth, let it fill with air, then sealed her lips. She pressed her mouth against Sara's. Once their lips were sealed against one another's, Clara opened her mouth just enough for the air to escape. Sara withdrew, her lips sealed. She climbed down the ladder and pressed her mouth against Roy's. They repeated the process. Roy walked a length of the tunnel and pressed his mouth against Jack's. Jack walked a further length of the tunnel and pressed his mouth against Ashley's. Ashley walked a further length of the tunnel and pressed her mouth against Anthony. Anthony walked a length of the tunnel and pressed his mouth against Danny's. Danny walked a length of the tunnel and pressed his mouth again Gauri's. Gauri walked a length of the tunnel and pressed her mouth against Lydia's. This went on until the small pocket of air finally reached Susie, who pressed her mouth against Sam's. Her cheeks went red. Sam thought he could taste Clara.

He hardly ever saw her anymore. He was getting farther and farther away from her, but he could not stop digging. She was there, as nearly everyone else was, to see where this was going.

The children dug for weeks, months. Jimmi, along with a few other parents, brought them food and water and comfortable materials on which they could sit or sleep. The parents watched their children work. It was a fine sight to see, them all working together. How dedicated they were, how focused. Every now and then one of the parents would erupt into a cheer or begin to applaud wildly. Some cried. One woman said over and over again, "I could not be prouder; I could not be more proud."

Jimmi brought gloves for Clara. He brought her a handkerchief. He held her small hands, which were rough with work.

"Do you mind if I'm here?" he asked. "Do you mind my watching?"

She did not mind, but she had to get back to work. The buckets of earth were coming steadily now, and there was no time to waste if they were going to get as much work done as they could before it was time for dinner, a shower, and bed.

Jimmi did not miss her, not really. But he still felt a sadness at the sight of her working alongside all of her friends. There was nothing he could do to help her. She did not need him here, not really. He could have been home, he realized, preparing a well-rounded dinner, or cleaning her room, which was dusty and streaked with mud. He could have been laying out her clothes, buying her new ones. In a way, it was selfish, his watching her, his admiring her from afar while she carried on, indifferent to his presence. Every now and then, though, when she returned from the woods with an empty bucket, or after she tied the bucket, lowered it over the hole's edge, she would look up, see him there, and she would wave. Just as casually, she would go back to work. But he was left with an immensely pleasurable feeling. He felt wine drunk, happy for her and for him. He felt full of purpose, sitting there on the quilt he'd brought for her, in case she got tired and needed to rest. She never did, though. She never rested. She was one of the hole's hardest workers.

The day the children began to faint, Jimmi had brought egg salad for all the parents, and any child tired enough to rest.

Some of the diggers fell first. Then some of the children carrying buckets. One child fell while climbing the ladder. He hit the bottom of the hole with a wet thud. Sam stopped digging when he heard the sounds, wet thuds all around him. He ran the length of the hole, climbed the ladder and said,

"Everybody's falling over."

Parents charged the mouth of the hole. They paced, waited, while a handful climbed down the single rope ladder. Clara returned from the woods to find Jimmi in a panic. He patted her down, touched her arms, her cheeks, the top of her head. He looked into her eyes, snapped his fingers. He blew in her face, and she flinched. He fell to his knees and kissed her hands, and she asked what was happening.

He didn't know, but some of the children had fallen. They were collapsing. Something was wrong.

"Is it the air?" she asked.

He didn't know.

Only six children fainted. Men carried them out of the hole, draped over their shoulders. They laid them out on the wood floor and ran for help while everyone gathered around them.

“Get back,” said one of the parents.

“We need a doctor,” said another.

“Somebody get a doctor,” said a third.

The children were exhausted. Even those that hadn’t fainted. They’d worked and worked and dug themselves a tremendous hole, but they were not able to keep up that rate of production. They’d rested when they’d needed to. They’d eaten well. They took care of themselves. But it was still too much. So they stopped. The hole remained. It could not be called incomplete. It was as much as it had ever been. A hole.

Sam returned Jimmi’s shovel. He asked to see Clara.

“Sure,” said Jimmi.

Clara was in her room. Jimmi told Sam to wait, he would go and get her.

In her room, Clara on the bed, coloring a stack of computer paper.

"Sam's here."

She looked up. She smiled at her father. He'd given her the computer paper. He'd given her the colored pens.

"I'm bored," she'd said.

When she colored, she did not stop for lines or distinct shapes. She let the pens wander the page. She got ink on her bedspread, ink on her hands. She filled the pages with movement.

"I'm really happy to see more of you at home," he said.

She looked back down at her coloring.

"I was starting to miss you, even though I still saw you every day."

She asked if Sam was coming in and Jimmi said he'd told him to wait a moment.

"I think Sam wants to take you away," Jimmi said.

She stopped coloring. She looked up.

"Take me somewhere else?"

"I think so."

"Can I go?"

"If you want."

"Do I want to?"

Jimmi shrugged.

"I think so," he said.

"Here." She gave him the stack of colored paper.

After she left, he covered the walls of the living room with the paper. It was purple and yellow and red and green and orange and blue and black and white. He phoned some of the neighbors every now and then. Their children were doing fine. He was glad to hear it. He wondered where Clara and Sam had gone but knew better than to wonder long. There was no way of knowing. And he did not want to know. It was for them, where they went. He would hear from her again. And even if he didn't, he would not forget her.

Her pages wilted in the summer heat. Sun through the windows stained them. He listened to music sometimes. Other times he did not. He started a garden that did not last. He grew much older. He grew a beard. She phoned him one afternoon, while he was sipping lemonade in what had been his garden.

"Hello," said his daughter.

"Hi, sweetie."

A bee landed on the back of his hand. He turned his palm down to consider it, and the bee left.

"Everything is incredible here," she said. "Except we're running low on money."

"Do you want me to send you some?"

She did not answer.

"How's Sam?"

"Sam is Sam," she said.

Jimmi smiled. She sounded happy and confident, like she knew the man so well.

"Sweetie," Jimmi said, "I'm going to die now."

"Okay," she said. "Did you see the bee?"

"Yes," he said, "And thank you."

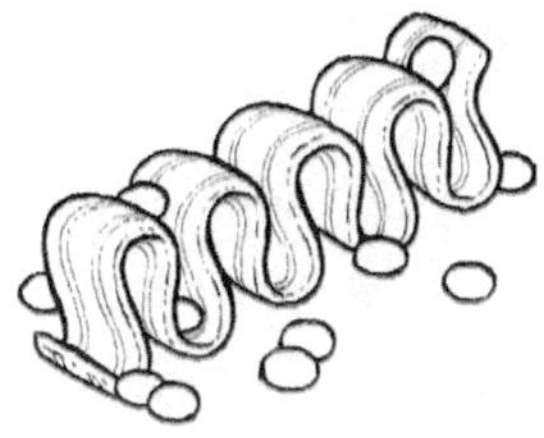

Clara and Sam did not go far. They bought a horse and named it Steel. They adopted a two-year-old girl named Bonnie. They held Bonnie up in front of Steel and let her touch his nose. The horse chuffed and Bonnie squealed and hit her hands together.

Their house was small, but on a good amount of land. Sam rode Steel in the mornings. He filled a barn with wire and cotton and sheet metal, which he coiled into balls and rolled out to various places in one of the open fields on their property. Partly so he could jump Steel over the various obstacles, but mainly because he liked the look of them. They were gnarled and unfriendly looking from one angle, and from another they reflected the sky, the grass, the oncoming horse and rider.

Clara swam in a small pond by the barn. She bathed Bonnie in the sink. They opened a small store on Main Street. They sold food items, some souvenirs. Arrowheads and ponchos. They sold peach preserves Clara made from the orchard she'd discovered the first summer of their living together. They made just enough money to be comfortable, and to raise Bonnie. They did not need much. They lived simply. They ordered food for the store and ate a lot of what they did not sell. When Sam got sick, Clara ran the store by herself. None of the customers seemed to mind the young child on her knee, at her side, on the floor.

They buried Sam on their property, a few yards from the dock leading out over the pond. A minister came, though they were not religious. There were very few clouds in the sky. A large puffy one. One that looked like a star. Clara pointed that cloud out to Bonnie.

"That is your father," she said.

Bonnie squealed, hit her hands together.

At night, Clara told Bonnie stories about Sam, her father. She wanted the child to grow up in his presence, or some semblance of his presence. At first, the stories were mostly true: how they'd met, things they'd done together, the hole they'd dug together, how Sam had proposed, those kinds of things. But Clara began to have vivid dreams, their nights were so peaceful and quiet out on the ranch together, and she weaved elements of those dreams into her stories.

"Your father and I had met many times before we met in this life. We were friends, lovers, teacher and student, we have known each other for many lives." Clara's dreams were startlingly real. She saw herself as practicing the art of lucid dreaming. She pushed for what she considered to be visions, past-life regressions. "I knew your father as a healer in a village many many centuries ago. I went to him. He held my wrist, and the pain was lifted."

When she woke from these dreams, in the silver haze that encompassed their ranch home at night, she was always disoriented, confused, frightened, and eventually disappointed. She lived several lives alongside Sam in her dreams, each one just as real as the next. When she woke, she was completely alone.

Bonnie grew older. She lost her teeth. She grew new ones. She was muscular, rugged. She got cuts, bruises, rashes from various plants. She ignored them, and they healed. She learned to brush Steel, and eventually to ride him. By the time she was eight, she was taking early morning rides around the property, into the woods and far out of sight of her mother, who sat on the porch and considered their property. Bonnie arrived home from her rides, sweaty and eager to let the day begin. Steel looked stronger than ever. He was slick with oil and sap from the wooded ride. Bonnie's legs were often littered with cuts. Clara smiled to see them. She took naps throughout the day. She lay in bed, her eyes closed. She waited for the next dream, the next vision. In one, she was a hunter. In one, she witnessed Noah building the ark. She built an ark of her own, along with a team of builders. Sam was there, three nails held between his teeth. They had to hurry; storm clouds were gathering.

Bonnie grew up. She worked regular hours at the store. She attended high school, did well, was well liked. She was driven in almost everything by curiosity. She sought out intimate friendships because she was curious about people. She studied. She read. She rode Steel and explored their property, the surrounding properties. She brought Steel by the front porch, every morning, where Clara would sit and sip water or nothing and wave to her daughter as she disappeared over the hills and into the woods. Clara sat alone and dreamed while Bonnie was out. Clara dreamed she was on the beach, prone in the sand. She rose, walked to the highway. Woods surrounded her. A car approached from behind and pulled over. Sam sat at the wheel. He offered her a ride. A breeze passed through the woods around her, and the trees all seemed to shift, to shudder. They leaned into one another. Just then, Bonnie climbed out of the passenger's seat. She looked over at Clara from across the bed of the truck. Clara began to speak, but Bonnie turned. She entered the woods and disappeared. Clara climbed into what had been Bonnie's seat in the truck. Sam and Clara drove on together. The road, the woods, the car melted away. It was just the two of them, and the sun. They entered the light and fell together. There was little heat. There was wind all around them. Clara felt Sam's hands and the wind and the light of the sun and some part of her finally released. A tension in her shoulders, a tightness she'd been holding for years. Her vertebrae settled, collapsing the space between them, one by one. Slowly, she grew thin and small. Eventually, she vanished.

The woods grew thick around Bonnie. Steel was apprehensive, as she'd never seen him. The trees grew closer together, clung to her legs, Steel's sides. She pushed him on. He paused; she pressed him with her calves. She was not sure anymore, which way was home. The tops of the trees bent toward one another and began to join, to tangle, as if grappling with one another, as if each was trying to pull the other down. She dismounted, took Steel by the reins and led him through the tangled and tangling trees. Finally, she squeezed between the trunks of two enormous cedars, but Steel's shoulders could not fit. He could not move forward. She tied the reins to one of the trees. She told herself she was lost. She told herself she needed to walk on, to continue forward until she reached something recognizable, something familiar.

Eventually, she came upon a hole. A hole in the earth that was darker than the light would go. A rope ladder hung from the edge. Curious, she climbed down. She climbed lower and lower until she was exhausted with climbing. She looked down but couldn't see a bottom. She only saw the faint light on the walls around her. She could see the vague white of her hands on the ropes in front of her. She saw the ring of light above her. She continued until her arms were weak and she could move no further. She hung a moment, draped her arms over a rung of the ladder. She breathed a moment. Her knees buckled. She fell.

She hit the ground after only a moment and collapsed. The dirt was moist. It clung to her arms, her cheeks and hair. She rose up and considered the ring of light above her. There was no way she could climb back up, not right away. Her arms were drained. Her body was sore and frail. She'd been riding, walking, climbing for hours. For what seemed like forever. She patted the walls around her, measured the size of the space. Before she could make a full circle, though, she discovered an opening in the wall, across from where she remembered the ladder being. She kept her right hand on the wall at her side and moved down the corridor. The earth gave beneath her trailing hand. She felt herself dragging slivers into the dirt wall, little canals. She fingered the slick edge of what might have been an earthworm. She felt small roots bend to her touch. She felt the dirt build up beneath her fingernails. She walked on, one heavy step after the next. She thought of her mother. She thought of what it might be like, to live one's life in pursuit of a dream. Not a hope, not a fantasy, but the act of dreaming. An abandonment of oneself to fantasy, to the imagined. For years she had avoided her mother, if only because she felt her mother sought to avoid her. Bonnie rode her horse. She stayed out late, kissed boys, let them touch her, touched them. She stole from their shop, little things, necklaces or candy. Her fingers trailed in the dirt of the wall. She felt disoriented, unsure of each step, but that did not slow her. She walked deeper and deeper. The strength came back to her legs. She felt like she could walk for as long as she would need to, for the entire length of this hole. What she would do then, she did not know. She might sleep. She needed sleep, she knew that. Clara's hand would come up when Bonnie returned. She could walk for as long as she would need to.

Clara kissed her eyelids, even now. Not every night, but every once in a while. The dirt coiled along her fingertips as she dragged them. She drew clump after clump of raw mud from the wall, dropped them at her feet. She left a little trail of wet clumps. Water dribbled from the holes she made, collected at her feet. Her mother would never be happy, because she believed so wholly in what she could only imagine. Her mind would never shut off the idea of something different, something greater, something holding together all of what little they had. Bonnie felt sorry for her. Bonnie wanted to cry. Step after step, she thought about crying. She moved and the hole seemed to grow with each step. There was no light. She could see nothing at all. Nothing but the textured haze of darkness. Blues and reds, yellows and greens, humming. She was more and more a part of their absence. She couldn't picture light, not exactly. Water lapped the edges of her feet. She remembered Steel. The way he'd looked when she left him. The reins tied to the branch of a cedar tree. The look in his eyes. She'd expected him to look hurt, but he hadn't. His eyes were wet, but they were always wet. He shook the muscles along his back and sides. He pawed at the ground. He looked around, in every direction he was able to turn. She'd walked away from him, looked back once or twice. And he was there each time, looking as he had the moment before, shaking and turning this way and that. He made a few sounds she recognized: a whinny, a chuff. He tapped his teeth. He made one sound she did not recognize, a kind of cough. A kind of sigh or strained breath. She turned and walked in the direction she had set for herself. She took step after heavy step, her hand trailing in the mud, the water coming. His hoof came down, and he curled his leg back up.

Just outside of town, there was a creek. A thin thing, with little power behind it, hidden beneath a coat of tall grass. Passing by, passing over, one could hear it before it came into view. The sound of running water filled that stretch of land. Though faint, it could be heard for a good distance in any direction. The creek was miles from a hydroelectric dam. The dam had a small leak at its base. Over time, the foundation had shifted, the concrete began to crack. As the crack grew, the foundation weakened. The creek's source was that quarter-inch crack in the foundation of the hydroelectric dam. It wasn't long before the town discovered the leak. But they were losing very little power to it. At the time, it was cheaper to leave the crack, to keep an eye on its growth, rather than to redo the foundation. Cheaper, easier.

They did not really keep an eye on the crack. It grew. It went unnoticed. People flipped switches. They took hot showers.

They charged their phones, their computers. They cooked dinners on electric stoves, microwaved gravy and leftovers.

Joe flipped a breaker, the lights in the house went out. He flipped it again, and everything lit. He heard the buzz of the microwave, the glug of the fish tank's filter. His house was empty, the electronics around him hummed.

His house was swarming with insects. He'd left the window open all through the night. He'd left the lights on, the garage door open, and when he'd clicked on the lamp at his bedside that night, the power had shut off completely. The bugs had died down. There was an intense silence all around. His ears roared.

Coming back from flipping the breaker, he found the insects active again. Mayflies and moths, beetles and winged ants, they flew around him, investigated his ears. They landed on his shoulders, his arms. He poured himself a glass of water, considered the plug in the center of the room. Most of his lights and kitchen appliances ran from a single surge protector in the center of the room. Extension cords snaked out and down the hall, splitting off into the rooms that needed lamps, outlets: his bedroom, the bathroom, his study. The fish moved in their tank as the insects did around his kitchen table, in broken figure eights, fast then slow. They pulsed. June bugs struck the table dumbly. They flipped, kicked their ratcheting arms and legs. Their wings buzzed. Joe's family had grown up and out of the house like vines.

After they left, Joe began remodeling the house. He took down a few walls, tried to rewire the bedrooms and the living room. He was "opening the house up" as he put it. But the place was a mess. A tangle of extension cords and dust.

His daughter's rooms he left untouched. There were only a few things left anyway. Sheets, pillows, a few toys they cared so little about they'd been willing to leave them when they left. His wife had taken everything. Everything except for a mirror they'd had mounted to the bedroom wall. That's not to say she didn't try. That's not to say she wasn't making plans to have it removed.

Joe hung clothes from the edges of the mirror. He obscured it with electrical tape but made sure to use the kind that wouldn't leave streaks.

He was napping when the water trickled in. It came in under the door, soaked into the rug. It made a soft sound as it ran across the wood floor, soaked into the bags of tools he'd left out, the paper towels he'd dropped earlier in the night and let roll to a stop in the middle of what had been the living the room.

A siren sounded when the water was already a foot or so deep. It lifted an end table, knocked it against the bedroom door. Joe sat up in bed, threw his legs over the side and plunged them into the water. He gathered himself into the center of the bed. The flood siren wailed. The water reached the top of the bed and soaked into the sheets, the comforter. It slid over the top of the bed to meet itself in the center. Joe got off the bed and stepped into the water. He knocked smooth objects with his feet. He opened the bedroom door, more water poured in. The house was filling, was full, was empty. He opened the front door and water poured in. He lifted the phone from its receiver, heard nothing, and dropped it into the waist-high water. He realized he hadn't yet made a sound. He screamed, nothing in particular. He just made sound at the water. In response, it rose around him.

Joe had seen images of floods before, and in them, people were always gathered on their rooftops, signaling for help or being saved. He pulled down the hidden ladder to the attic, let it drop into the water. He climbed into the dusty crawl space and made his way to a vent on the far side of the house. The house was empty of insects. They'd abandoned him. He kicked out the vent and it made a soft splash in the water below. He drew his upper body out first, clung to the edge of the roof with both hands. Then he pulled his lower body to the edge of the vent's frame. It bent beneath his feet as he pulled himself up and onto the roof. The shingles scraped his soft, wet feet. He looked out, for miles there was nothing but water, and trees and houses. He saw no people, no animals but a few birds. They moved as they always had, indifferent to what was happening below.

Joe sat on the roof. He watched the birds. Only a few passed. He watched the water. It rose, slowly, surely. It grew. He thought of his wife but didn't know what to think. Maybe she had made it to her roof as well.

The siren wailed. Joe sat on his roof. The water rose, and he yelled.

He yelled and he yelled. But there was no one. He prayed, asked for forgiveness. The water did not stop. If he survived, he would call his wife, his daughters. He would apologize. Not for one thing, but for everything. He didn't know where he would begin, but he would. It was hard to think of one thing in particular that had gone wrong, but things hadn't been right. Joe ignored it, the ever-present feeling that he could be doing something different, should be doing something different. He'd never done anything other than what he'd wanted to do, and people had always loved him for it. People had always loved him without question, and he couldn't think of a single thing he'd ever done to deserve it. And still, he felt he deserved it. He spent more time alone. The feeling did not go away. And eventually, his wife left. His daughters had been sad, maybe, but they had not fought the decision. They'd cried and packed their bags.

Water filled the gutters, made a thin metal ringing. He heard the house groan, felt it move, felt it shudder. At first, he paced—one far side of the roof to the other. Then he sat, brought his knees to his chest. He put the side of his right wrist against his mouth, spread his lips, and took that part of his arm between his teeth. He sucked his wrist and watched the water rise.

When the water reached the roof, Joe saw a pillow floating just a short distance from him. The pillowcase was white with blue and yellow cartoon flowers. Water lapped the edge of the roof. He rose and went to the roof's edge. Water in every direction. Treetops jutted out, broke the swaying green of the water's surface. There were no more birds. The sun, too, was nearly gone. The sky was golden but growing dark. It fell to bronze. The water looked dark, darker with each passing moment. He leaned, reached for the pillow, but it was just beyond his fingers. It was dry on top, but gradually retaining water, slowly sinking. He looked around as if a stick or pole might be waiting for him somewhere in an unexamined corner of his barren roof.

He leapt into the water. His head broke the surface, and he looked in every direction for the flower pillow. It moved from him with the ripples his body caused. He reached out again, missed, splashed it a bit further. The sky was dark now, the water too. The pillow went under. He turned himself downward to swim after it. He opened his eyes and could see only the dark gold of the water. He turned, turned again. Nothing. He swam a bit deeper. His cheeks were puffed and rounded with air. He pictured his wife sitting atop the roof of her new apartment complex. She was there in a rocking chair. His daughters would have been at gymnastics practice. Maybe she'd driven to save them. Maybe they were in the car, floating atop the river, on their way to safety. Somewhere near him, the pillow sank deeper. He swam. He reached out for it. He felt he could swim forever.

After the flood, the city repaired the dam. Many made it out just fine. Others didn't. They rebuilt the city. They rebuilt homes. Some homes. But years later, the place looked better than ever. They added a new movie theater, a water park. They rebuilt the courthouse in the center of the town square.

On the day of the courthouse's completion, the mayor of Gainesville, Kyle Garret, gathered the people together in the square. He lifted the microphone from its stand, surveyed the audience, and began.

"We all suffered a great loss. Losses, really. We lost friends, family, homes. I can't speak to the unimaginable grief we all experienced only a few years ago. But I ask you, on this day, I ask you to remember, that we have not lost everything. You look around you and you see that we have not lost everything. What we've lost will never be forgotten. But we must also remember what we have. We have one another. Look around you. We have a community. We've grown up and out of what might have been the greatest tragedy of our lives. And together, we rebuild. All it takes is the dream," he said, "to rebuild."

It was twilight. Slowly, the streetlights lit. People cheered when the speech ended. They clapped and yelled and embraced one another. Children ran between the legs of their parents. The grass grew. There was an armed robbery and the fireflies stirred. A fight broke out. A condom broke. A man raised his hand, and a woman raised her hand. The wheels of the new projectors began to roll. Two strangers fell in love, made coffee. Children filled water guns with urine, and someone made a move. Someone clutched her leg, her arm. A movie ended with a confession, with forgiveness, with love. Credits rolled. *Filmed on location*, they said, *in Gainesville, Texas.*

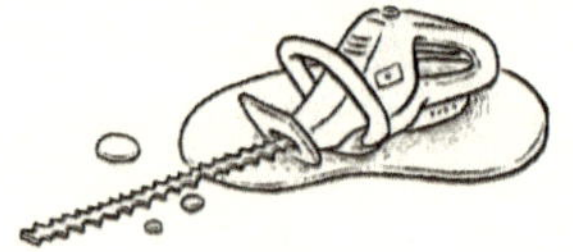

Colin Winnette is the author of several books, including *The Job of the Wasp* (long-listed for *The Believer* Book Award) and the indie best-seller *Coyote*. His novel *Users* was called the "first great novel about virtual reality" by *The Nation*. It was a Finalist for the 2024 Pen/Faulkner Award for Fiction, a *New York Times* Editor's Choice Pick, and a *New Yorker* Best Book of 2023. Winnette lives in San Francisco and can be found online at colinwinnette.com.

Long Day Press

New & Forthcoming Titles

An Atavic Fear of Hailstorms
João Reis
Novella
ISBN: 9781950987290 • $14

Girl Thing
Morghen Tidd
Stories
ISBN: 9781950987368 • $16

Saturn
Simon Jacobs
Stories
ISBN: 9781950987481 • $16

We Go Liquid
Christian TeBordo
Novel
ISBN: 9781950987412 • $16

LongDayPress.com @LongDayPress

Avoid alcohol
CLOSE
OPEN
Push down & turn

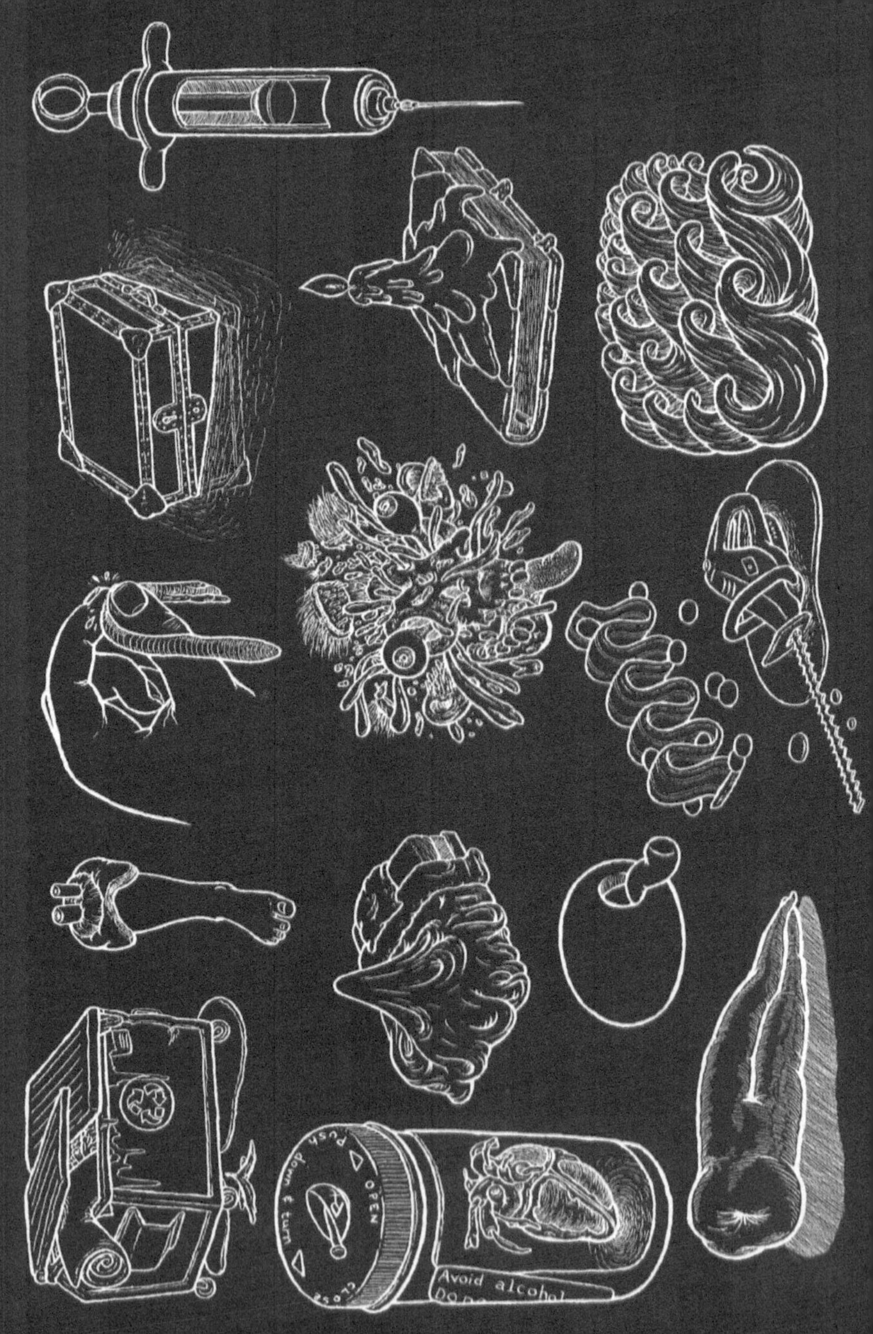
push down & turn
OPEN
close
Avoid alcohol

www.ingramcontent.com/pod-product-compliance
Lightning Source LLC
Chambersburg PA
CBHW021726190726
48289CB00008B/2717

* 9 7 8 1 9 5 0 9 8 7 4 7 4 *